Welcome to Penhally Bay!

Nestled on the rugged Cornish coast is the picturesque town of Penhally. With sandy beaches, breathtaking landscapes and a warm, bustling community—it is the lucky tourist who stumbles upon this little haven.

But now Mills & Boon® Medical™ Romance is giving readers the unique opportunity to visit this fictional coastal town through our brand-new twelve-book continuity… You are welcomed to a town where the fishing boats bob up and down in the bay, surfers wait expectantly for the waves, friendly faces line the cobbled streets and romance flutters on the Cornish sea breeze…

We introduce you to Penhally Bay Surgery, where you can meet the team led by caring and commanding Dr Nick Tremayne. Each book will bring you an emotional, tempting romance—from Mediterranean heroes to a sheikh with a guarded heart. There's royal scandal that leads to marriage for a baby's sake, and handsome playboys are tamed by their blushing brides! Top-notch city surgeons win adoring smiles from the community, and little miracle babies will warm your hearts. But that's not all…

With Penhally Bay you get double the reading pleasure…as each book also follows the life of damaged hero Dr Nick Tremayne. His story will pierce your heart—a tale of lost love and the torment of forbidden romance. Dr Nick's unquestionable, unrelenting skill would leave any patient happy in the knowledge that she's in safe hands, and is a testament to the ability and dedication of all the staff at Penhally Bay Surgery. Come in and meet them for yourself…

Dear Reader

I have always believed that trust is one of the most important ingredients for a successful relationship—especially in a marriage. It would be impossible to commit yourself to share a life with another person if you didn't know, without a shadow of a doubt, that they would always have your best interests at heart.

This is a dilemma that confronts Maggie Pascoe when she meets up again with Adam Donnelly in the third book of the *Brides of Penhally Bay* series, commissioned especially for the Mills & Boon centenary year. The last time Maggie saw Adam he broke her heart—and the bond of trust that had existed since she'd fallen in love with him when they were teenagers. Within hours disaster strikes, and the only way Maggie can survive her worst nightmare is if she can learn to trust him all over again, to believe that he will do everything in his power to bring her back where she belongs…in his arms.

Maggie and Adam's story is especially close to my heart. Not only because it is set in the magical county where I live, but also because I share Maggie's phobia and needed to trust my own special hero to hold my hand while I went underground to research this part of Cornwall's heritage. I hope you enjoy discovering it too.

Happy reading

Josie

THE DOCTOR'S BRIDE BY SUNRISE

BY
JOSIE METCALFE

MILLS & BOON®
Pure reading pleasure™

First published in Great Britain 2007
Large Print edition 2008
Harlequin Mills & Boon Limited,
Eton House, 18-24 Paradise Road,
Richmond, Surrey TW9 1SR

© Josie Metcalfe 2007

ISBN: 978 0 263 19968 0

Set in Times Roman 16¾ on 19 pt.
17-0808-50957

Printed and bound in Great Britain
by Antony Rowe Ltd, Chippenham, Wiltshire

Josie Metcalfe lives in Cornwall with her long-suffering husband. They have four children. When she was an army brat, frequently on the move, books became the only friends that came with her wherever she went. Now that she writes them herself she is making new friends, and hates saying goodbye at the end of a book—but there are always more characters in her head, clamouring for attention until she can't wait to tell their stories.

Recent titles by the same author:

TWINS FOR A CHRISTMAS BRIDE
A MARRIAGE MEANT TO BE
SHEIKH SURGEON, SURPRISE BRIDE
A FAMILY TO COME HOME TO
A VERY SPECIAL PROPOSAL

BRIDES OF PENHALLY BAY

Bachelor doctors become husbands and fathers—
in a place where hearts are made whole.

In June we met pregnant Lucy Tremayne
when she is reunited with the man she loves
Christmas Eve Baby by Caroline Anderson

Then we snuggled up with gorgeous Italian, Dr Avanti
The Italian's New-Year Marriage Wish by Sarah Morgan

Now romance blossoms for Adam and Maggie
The Doctor's Bride by Sunrise by Josie Metcalfe

Single dad Jack Tremayne finds his perfect bride
in book four
The Surgeon's Fatherhood Surprise by Jennifer Taylor

In book five a princess arrives in Penhally!
The Doctor's Royal Love-Child by Kate Hardy

In book six Edward Tremayne
finds the woman of his dreams
Nurse Bride, Bayside Wedding by Gill Sanderson

Book seven sees gorgeous Chief Inspector
Lachlan D'Ancey's wedding
Single Dad Seeks a Wife by Melanie Milburne

The temperature really hots up
when Dr Oliver Fawkner arrives in the Bay…
Virgin Midwife, Playboy Doctor by Margaret McDonagh

In book nine Francesca and Mike try one last time
for the baby they've longed for
Their Miracle Baby by Caroline Anderson

Book ten brings sexy Sheikh Zayed
to the beaches of Penhally
Sheikh Surgeon Claims His Bride by Josie Metcalfe

Snuggle up with dishy Dr Tom Cornish in book eleven
A Baby for Eve by Maggie Kingsley

And don't miss French doctor Gabriel, who sweeps into
the Bay in the twelfth *Brides of Penhally Bay* book
Dr Devereux's Proposal by Margaret McDonagh

A collection to treasure for ever!

CHAPTER ONE

'PULL over, Mike…fast! I've lost him,' Maggie said tersely as the monitor shrilled a warning.

Automatically, she braced herself as the ambulance veered off the road and onto a rutted verge then jerked to a halt, but her concentration was focused entirely on Walter Dinnis and the fact that he no longer had a pulse.

With the ease of too much practice she delivered a precordial thump to the centre of his chest and began the compressions that would keep oxygenated blood circulating around his brain and vital organs, knowing that Mike would be joining her at any moment.

The back doors swung open and her fellow ambulance officer leapt in to join her, positioning himself to take over cardiac thrusts on their elderly patient without needing to be asked. That left her free to peel the gel off the backing strips and position them on the retired fisherman's skinny chest, ready for the electrodes.

'Prepare to shock,' bleated the automated voice, and Mike held both hands clear while the machine discharged 200 joules through the uselessly quivering heart.

'Damn! Back into v-fib. No viable rhythm,' Maggie muttered under her breath. 'Come on, Walter. You can do it,' she said encouragingly as the machine charged up again, the high-pitched whine still audible over the sound of Mike's rhythmic counting as he performed the lifesaving thrusts. 'Two hundred again, Mike. Clear!'

The jagged trace returned again without any semblance of order, telling them both that there was no blood being pumped into any of the elderly man's vital organs.

'No! Don't *do* this!' she said fiercely, an image in her head of the white face of his terror-stricken wife watching them take her husband away. Betty would be following them at any moment in their daughter's car and the last thing she needed was to come up the hill out of Penhally and find the ambulance pulled up at the side of the road. The man had survived working his whole life in one of the most dangerous professions in the world…he'd been a familiar figure around Penhally all her life…and it all came down to this moment.

'You're *not* going to die on me!' she told him fiercely. 'Charging to 360 and…clear!'

The wiry body arched up alarmingly as the jolt of electricity was discharged into his heart, but this time, after several seconds of ominous silence, the blessed sound of sinus rhythm was restored.

'And make sure it stays that way, Walter, or Betty will never forgive me,' Maggie muttered sternly to her patient as Mike closed the doors again and made his way back to the driving seat. She folded the printout strip detailing the successful attempt at cardioversion into Walter's file. 'Let's get him to St Piran's…asap!' she suggested with a swift glance towards her colleague.

Out of the corner of the windscreen she caught sight of a jumble of bright colours behind some gorse bushes and turned her focus on them with a frown. It wasn't until Mike was pulling back onto the road that she suddenly realised what it was she'd been looking at.

'A kid's bicycle…that's what it was,' she whispered under her breath, then smiled when she turned back to check Walter's oxygen perfusion, glad to see that it was once more above ninety per cent and he was conscious again.

The expression in his eyes was dazed and confused and she quickly set about reassuring him, but at the same time the image of that brightly painted bike against the sere winter grass stayed with her.

In fact, now that she thought about it, there had been more than one of them in the field behind the high stone wall, and she wondered idly what they were doing this far out of Penhally. The road was steep and winding and the riders would definitely have had to walk their bikes for most of the distance—no mean feat for a youngster.

By the size of the bikes, the children they belonged to weren't very old but, then, this was half-term week for all the local schools and the whole group of them was probably exploring or building some sort of den in the corner of one of the fields or under one of the familiar trees that had been permanently deformed by the sharp bite of winter gales and the prevailing winds.

At that age, the youngsters were unlikely to be up to anything dangerous, but they could definitely be up to mischief if the traditional holiday-time rise in callouts was anything to go by. In spite of the fact that it was still mid-February, they'd already had to transport one lad injured in a fall on the rocks below the light-house and another rescued from an unplanned swim off the harbour wall at half-tide.

Walter's heart behaved itself for the rest of their journey and as they did a speedy handover at St Piran's A and E, Maggie marvelled at the way a brain could function on so many levels at once. Especially a female brain, they'd been told during one set of lectures during her paramedic training. The males in the room had jeered, but she'd proved it time and again when a male colleague had been concentrating on monitoring one set of injuries, only to completely lose track of other emerging symptoms.

She had certainly tried to make sure that she kept her standards up, trying not to miss anything significant, no matter how small, but that didn't stop her brain from cataloguing something extraneous…such as those bicycles…and filing it away.

Now they were on the return journey, providing unofficial transport back to Penhally for Maureen, another ambulance service worker, who'd been released after day-case surgery for the repair of an inguinal hernia.

And there were those bikes again, still there behind the gorse bushes, even though it was getting dark.

'Some kids are going to be in trouble with their mums when they get back late tonight,' she murmured under her breath, while Mike and Maureen chatted with the ease of long-time colleagues.

She could easily understand how the time could get away from the youngsters while they were enjoying themselves, with the February nights still drawing in far too fast, but she could all too easily sympathise with the mothers who would be worrying about them. These narrow roads weren't ideal for cycling at any time of the day, but after dark they could be lethal, few of them having any street lighting once you left the town itself.

'Door to door, ladies,' Mike announced as he drew up in a parking space outside the surgery and hopped out to unlock the double doors at the back of the ambulance with a flourish before dropping the steps. 'Come on, gorgeous. Time to get home and put your feet up while the old man makes you some tea.' He leant a little closer and added, 'And you tell him the surgeon said he's not allowed to get fruity until you've had your check-up.'

'You watch it, Mike Barber, or I'll tell Brian what you said,' Maureen warned, but there was a gleam of humour in her eyes. Her years in the service, first as a technician, like Mike, then as office staff, when the children had started arriving, had obviously taught her not to take any nonsense. 'My Brian'll soon sort your cheek out.'

'You know he would, too,' Maggie commented, when the older woman had walked gingerly across the car park to where her husband was waiting next door outside the front of Althorp's with a car full of children. 'And you wouldn't want to be messing with someone Brian's size. Have you seen the muscles on him? It must be something to do with all that physical labour in the boatyard.'

'I've got plenty of muscles of my own,' Mike pointed out, flexing his biceps inside his grass-green uniform, stung by what he obviously saw as a slight on his manhood.

'Yeah.' She hid her grin when he rose to the bait, the way he always did, 'But you buy *those* sorts of muscles with a few months of gym membership. *His* are the real thing, built up over a lifetime of use.'

She continued tidying the last few items away before they locked up and set off back to the depot for the end of their shift. With any luck they wouldn't have another callout before it was time to clean out their vehicle and hand over for the night.

'Hey, Maggie! Mike!' called a voice just as the two of them were walking forward to the cab.

'Mrs Furse…hello,' Maggie called back, then walked towards the motherly figure when she beckoned, pleased to see someone who had been one of her own mother's dearest friends.

'How many times do I have to tell you to call me Hazel now that you're all grown up?' she chided, giving Maggie a swift hug. 'I haven't seen the two of you for weeks, except for fleeting glimpses as you've been on the road somewhere, so I'm glad I caught you. Have you got to leave straight away or have you got time to come in for a drink? You really ought to meet our new locum. He's—'

'A drink, Hazel?' Mike interrupted gleefully. 'You wicked woman. What are you suggesting?'

'Tea, coffee or water, Mike Barber, as you very well know,' the practice's head receptionist said quellingly. 'And you behave yourself or I'll be having a word with your mother.'

He pulled a face. 'That's put me properly in my place...one of the penalties of living in the same town all your life.'

'But it can't be too bad a place if so many people want to come back here to live. Dr Nick, for example,' Maggie pointed out, as they followed Hazel up the stairs to the staffroom, trying to take her mind off what was about to happen. It wasn't an accident that they hadn't called in at the practice over the last two and a half weeks. It had been a deliberate ploy on her part to put off as long as possible the meeting that would bring back one of the most distressing days of her life.

'Nick's far from the only one to come back— there's also our newest recruit to the practice. He's an old Penhally boy, too,' Hazel said with a broad smile for someone who had just followed them into the room. 'Maggie, I don't know whether you'll remember him from when you were both at school here. He would have been several years above you. It's—'

'Adam Donnelly,' she whispered with her heart in her throat when she met those serious dark eyes for the first time in more than a year.

He was wearing a smart charcoal-grey suit that made him look every inch the respectable GP, but the shirt wasn't commonplace white but a clear blue that drew attention to the almost navy blue of his eyes. Had he remembered that she'd been the one to tell him that would happen?

At least she'd never been silly enough to tell him just how much those deep blue eyes had always affected her. That had been one of her secrets, as was the fact that she'd been head over heels in love with him long before he'd disappeared off to medical school.

Unfortunately, even though she tried to force herself not to react, those dark eyes still elicited the same response they always had…for all the good it would do her.

'Maggie,' he said with a nod of acknowledgement, but that single word in that unforgettable husky voice was enough to rip all the scars wide open again. The last time she'd heard it she'd been wrapped in his arms, believing…

'My goodness, you've got good memories!' Hazel exclaimed. 'You can't have seen each other since Adam went away to medical school, because his mother moved away from Penhally after… Oh, it must be ten years or so ago,' she finished hastily, clearly uncomfortable that she'd all but brought up the storm when Adam's father had been one of those who had died.

'We have met since then, Hazel,' Maggie said, taking pity on the poor woman's embarrassment. She held Adam's gaze deliberately as she continued lightly, 'We happened to bump into each other one day about a year ago when I went up to London to do one of my courses.' Nonchalant, that was what she'd been aiming for, but however it sounded it was better if everything was out in the open. After all, if she had known then that he…

'And then we got involved when there was an

accident on the underground,' Adam added, but his casual tone sounded far more genuine than her own. 'We were on the spot and were able to provide some assistance until the people with the proper equipment could arrive.'

Maggie marvelled that he could make the whole incident sound so inconsequential. It had given her nightmares for months as she'd relived every second of…

'So, people, is it tea or coffee today?' Hazel asked as she bustled across to the kitchenette to fill the kettle. 'And there might even be some biscuits left in the tin as Nick's been out on patient visits all afternoon.'

Maggie had been waiting for her chance to refuse, but the mention of Hazel's biscuits changed her mind in a hurry.

'What sort of biscuits? Your special Cornish fairings?' she asked, eager for a taste so reminiscent of the happier days of her childhood. 'I'd love one.'

'If you've got some spare, I wouldn't mind having one, too, Hazel,' said the elegant older man on the other side of the room as he looked up from scanning a handful of envelopes by the practice mail rack. 'Your famous biscuits are one reason why I agreed to come out of retirement to help young Nick when the Avantis went back to Italy and he didn't have enough staff to run the practice properly.'

'It's very kind of you to say so, Dr Fletcher,' Hazel said with an extra wash of pink to her cheeks. 'The Cornish fairings *are* Nick's favourites,' she added with a happy smile as she gave the tin an experimental shake then opened it.

'They're fast becoming my favourites, too,' Adam said with a grin as he managed to take two at once, and the mouthful Maggie had just taken turned to dust in her mouth at the unexpected glimpse of the grin that had captivated her right from the first time she'd seen it.

Then she'd been a lowly fifteen-year-old and Adam had been one of the seniors, heading into his last year at school. He'd been so far out of her orbit that he shouldn't have even noticed the skinny little girl staring at him while her heart had tried to beat its way out of her flat chest.

But he *had* noticed her and had sent her a grin exactly like the one he'd just sent to Hazel, and she'd been utterly captivated.

The whole of that year she'd spent haunting the corridors, hoping for a glimpse of him, and gradually from an easygoing grin their relationship had graduated through breathless pleasantries to actual conversations while they'd waited for the bus to take them to and from school.

By the time her sixteenth birthday had come around they'd confided so many secrets and ambitions to each other—including the fact that he was aiming for a career in medicine—but one thing she would always remember was the fact that it had been the day when Adam had kissed her for the first time.

Then he'd gone away to begin his training and, apart from that dreadful week when he'd returned to support his mother through the wait until his father's body had been found, then the heart-breaking memorial service that the whole of Penhally seemed to have attended, this was the first time Adam had ever returned to the town of his birth.

So, why now? she wondered as he and Mike discovered a mutual interest in the mining history of Cornwall. She couldn't imagine that the beautiful willowy blonde in their wedding photo would appreciate burying herself in a rural place like this. She was definitely a London person and would probably only feel at home in the more pretentiously exclusive corners of the county.

Well, at least I won't be called on to socialise with her, she thought, stifling the pang that her lack of choices over her career brought. She would have loved to have become a doctor, too—would have loved nothing more than to have followed Adam through medical school. But it wasn't to be. In her final year at school her mother had been diagnosed with cancer and there had been no way that she could have countenanced the idea of leaving the last beloved member of her family without support while

she underwent the gruelling rounds of chemotherapy, surgery and then more chemotherapy.

Still, Maggie couldn't imagine that a GP's
wife would be terribly keen to socialise with a
mere paramedic. Not that *she* saw her profession as inferior, just different. Paramedics were
often the first people to see a patient and it was
in their hands that patients' lives rested while
they were stabilised for transportation to
hospital. Far fewer accident victims would
survive were it not for the existence of paramedics. But even though she was proud of what
they were able to do for accident victims and of
the green uniform she wore, she had to admit
that they were still definitely from different
echelons in the medical hierarchy.

She managed to keep herself on the edge of
the conversation so that she didn't draw Hazel's
attention. She certainly didn't want to make it
obvious that she was avoiding speaking to
Adam, but just when she was trying to find a
way to edge towards the door unnoticed, there
was a disturbance somewhere out in the street.

'*Nick!*' screamed a woman's voice. '*Somebody! Help!*'

'That sounds almost like Kate Althorp,' Hazel said, her eyes wide. 'Oh, no! There must have been an accident in the boatyard.'

Adam and Mike were already heading for the stairs, their longer legs outstripping Maggie's so that she was playing catch-up by the time they reached the reception area.

'What's the matter, Kate?' Adam demanded, his eyes already beginning a primary survey of the white, shaking woman in front of him. 'Where are you hurt? Was it the machinery in the boatyard?'

'It's not me. It's Jem…' She held up her clenched fist and they saw the mobile phone for the first time. 'He rang me and said that there's been an accident and they're hurt.'

'What accident and who's hurt?' demanded Nick Tremayne, as he appeared from the direction of his consulting room, a bewildered patient following him into the hallway.

'Jem phoned me,' Kate said through chattering teeth, her whole body vibrating with the onset of shock. 'He's with some other boys. They went exploring and there's been a rockfall in a mine. They're hurt.'

'*Which* mine, Kate?' Nick had shouldered Adam aside and was gripping her shoulders in both hands now, as though he thought he could force her to hold herself together and concentrate. 'There are hundreds of the things all over Cornwall.'

'I *know* that, but I don't know which one!' she wailed. Maggie automatically stepped forward when she saw that the woman's knees were about to fail her, but Nick had the situation in hand, wrapping an arm around Kate and swiftly lowering her onto the nearest chair.

'You're wasting time, Kate. Stop yowling and *think*!' he said sharply, and they all heard her draw in a shocked breath, her dark eyes wide with hurt at his apparently brutal treatment. But his curtness obviously had the desired effect because she was no longer out of control.

'He didn't tell me *which* mine,' she said, tears

still streaming down her pale cheeks. 'And I tried to ring him back but the signal was too weak. You know how poor reception can be around here.' ◖

'Well, what *did* he say?' Nick demanded.

'That they were exploring in the mine and… and something…or some*one*…fell and they're hurt. Oh, God, Nick, he's hurt. My baby's hurt and I don't know where he is or—?'

'*They?*' Nick snapped. 'Who are *they*…his friends? *Who* are his friends? And where were they going to play?'

'They're…I don't know…' She shook her head. 'Some boys from the school, I think. He just waved goodbye to me and said he'd be back for tea and…and…' She nearly lost it again but there must have been something in Nick's face that forced her to hang onto her control. 'They looked a bit older than him, but he's so tall for his age… He only got his bike for Christmas and he's already starting to grow out of it and—'

'They were on bikes?' Maggie interrupted as an image suddenly leapt into her head, the one she'd spotted through the windscreen of the ambulance of a tangle of brightly coloured bicycle frames half-hidden behind some gorse bushes. 'Did you say there were four or five of them, all on bikes?'

'Yes! You saw them? Oh, Maggie, where were they? You could have brought them down to the surgery in the ambulance. Surely, if they were hurt, you could have—'

'Kate,' she interrupted gently, 'I didn't actually see any of the boys, but I'm almost certain that I know where their bikes are.' She turned towards her colleague. 'Mike, you remember where you had to stop the ambulance when Mr Dinnis…when I had to take care of Mr Dinnis?' Sometimes patient confidentiality could be a nuisance when you had to be so careful to watch every word. 'Well, I could see some gorse over the stone wall and there were several bikes there. I couldn't see how many but there were anything up to half a dozen.'

'Take me there, please!' Kate demanded, surging to her feet wild-eyed. 'I've got to find my son. He's all I've got left of…of…'

'You're not going anywhere until we've contacted the emergency services,' Nick said firmly, pressing her back into her seat. 'We need to—'

'I already dialled 999 and told them Jem was stuck down a mine.' It was Kate's turn to interrupt. 'They said they were going to send emergency services to Penhally…to meet up here, at the surgery…'

'That's because all our staff have done emergency rescue training…as you know well because you were the one to arrange it when you were practice manager,' Nick reminded her.

'In the meantime, I could go up the hill with Maggie and Mike and see if we can find out if we've got the right mine,' Adam suggested, and even as Maggie's brain registered that he'd had a good idea, her heart sank at the thought of being any closer to him than absolutely necessary.

She was still coming to terms with the fact that he was just as heart-breakingly handsome as ever and that he was for ever out of reach. The prospect of having to work with him on a regular basis wasn't something she wanted to contemplate.

In fact, it might be the only thing that could persuade her to move away from her beloved Penhally.

'Good idea, Adam,' Nick agreed, even though it was obvious that he would rather be the one in the thick of any activity. 'We'll wait to hear from you and lead the rescue teams up to you if Maggie's right.'

Maggie saw Mike beckoning her to the ambulance and realised that he'd gone out to take details from despatch of their next callout. If it was another heart-attack victim, like Walter Dinnis, she would have no option but to give Adam directions to the place she'd seen the bikes and leave him to find his own way. She was not in charge of determining priorities when the emergency calls came through and would have to go where she was told.

'That was Dispatch,' Mike confirmed. 'They know we're almost at the end of our shift but they're telling us to stay on duty here and do whatever we can until they can send out a re-placement crew to relieve us.'

'Shall I come with you?' Adam asked. 'Or would it be better if I followed you in my own vehicle?'

'It's your choice,' Maggie said briskly, grateful that if he were to come with them, he'd have to travel in the back of the vehicle. She didn't feel as if she was ready for any closer contact until she'd got her emotions a little better under control around him. It would be nice to know something simple…such as whether she loved him or loathed him after the way they'd parted a year ago.

'If you're coming with us you'll have to hop in the back and hang on—tight!' Mike called out. 'That twisting hill out of Penhally isn't comfortable at the best of times, and it's down-right evil in an ambulance.'

'I'll follow you in my car, then,' he said as Maggie double-checked that the back doors were firmly closed and raced towards the pas-senger door to climb into the cab.

* * *

Mike was already reversing the ungainly vehicle out of the surgery car park as Adam put the key in the ignition of his car, and when the ambulance driver gunned the powerful engine along the road edging the harbour, with blue lights and siren both going, Adam was surprised to see just how fast he was having to travel to keep up with them.

A middle-aged car driver tried to dispute priority as they approached the narrow bottleneck of Harbour Bridge but rapidly changed his mind when Mike flipped the headlights up full and drove straight at him. Adam had no difficulty following in his wake but at Higher Bridge they both had to slow down just long enough to negotiate the tight corner onto the narrow bridge with the massive granite parapets—they wouldn't be going anywhere if they sideswiped one of those—and then he could hear the full-throated roar of the engine that told him that Mike was using every ounce of power to pull up the winding road out of the steep-sided valley as quickly as possible.

Even though it had been years since he'd lived

in Penhally, the road was familiar enough that Adam could almost switch to automatic pilot to drive it, his thoughts centred on the woman travelling in the vehicle up ahead rather than on where they were going and why.

A major part of the reason why he'd signed on as a locum at Penhally Bay Surgery had been because Maggie still lived and worked in the area, but he'd been completely bowled over when he'd come into the staffroom a little while ago and found her standing there, the ultimate professional in her paramedic's uniform.

Her new hairstyle had been a bit of a shock, too. A year ago she'd still been wearing it in the same shoulder-length bob that he'd always known, tied back into a shiny dark ponytail for practicality, but he had to admit that the shorter style suited her elfin beauty even better, and highlighted all the colours that went to make her unusual hazel eyes.

He pulled a face when he replayed the expression on her face when she'd caught sight of him. It certainly hadn't been warmly welcoming but, then, what had he expected? He'd made a complete mess of things the last time he'd seen her and even though it had been unintentional, he knew he'd hurt her.

That was another reason why he was back in Penhally…to see if he could persuade her to listen while he explained exactly what had been going on in his chaotic life a year ago, to tell her that he hadn't deliberately set out to make her go against everything she believed in…that there had been extenuating circumstances that…

'Forget it for now,' he growled aloud when he saw the indicator signal that the vehicle ahead was going to pull off the road and slowed his own car ready to follow. 'There's nothing you can do about it until we find out where these kids are and what kind of help they need.'

Talking to Maggie, making her understand and, hopefully, getting her to forgive him and let him back into her life was why he was here, but that would all have to wait until he could persuade her to meet up with him after work.

For now he was going to have to switch his

brain into rescue mode and, as hard as it would be, he'd have to force himself to forget that the slender woman up ahead was anything other than a professional colleague.

CHAPTER TWO

'SLOW down a bit, Mike. I saw the bikes just up here on the left,' Maggie said, peering through the gathering gloom in attempt to spot the right clump of gorse bushes over the top of the stone wall, glad that they were nearly there.

Every second of the journey she'd been overwhelmingly aware that the car following in their wake was being driven by Adam Donnelly, the first man she'd ever loved and the one who'd broken her heart a year ago when they'd met up at that course in London.

He was absolutely the last person she'd expected to see walking into the staffroom at Penhally Bay Surgery at that time of day. She'd been certain that it would be safe...that he

would still have been out doing home visits…
and her instant reaction to those deep blue eyes
had been as visceral as ever.

She still didn't know whether she was horrified that she might have to deal with him on
occasion while he was a locum in the practice,
if she was called out to help one of his patients,
or whether she was delighted that he had reap-
peared in her life again.

What she did know was that every breath
she'd taken in his vicinity had drawn in the
unique mixture of soap and man that she'd
never been able to forget, and what was worse,
when he'd leaned towards her she'd been able
to feel his breath on her cheek and even ruffling
the hairs of her new, much shorter hairstyle.

'There's a gateway just a bit further on. I take
it that's the one we're looking for?' Mike said
as he indicated and swung the vehicle to a stop
just beyond where they'd halted a short while
ago. 'Can you—?' he began, but Maggie had
anticipated his request and was already out of
her seat, racing to open the gate.

'Are there any beasts in the field?' he called. 'Anything that could get out on the road and cause even more problems?'

'Nothing that I can see,' Maggie replied as she swung the gate wide and found the loose rock that the farmer had obviously left ready for use as a prop. 'But if you swing wide, we can use the headlights to make certain. Then I can leave this open.'

The wide swathe of light not only confirmed that the field was empty of any sheep or cows but also flashed across the jumble of bikes behind a sturdy growth of gorse.

'Yes! They're still there!' Maggie called. 'Did you see them?' She hurried across the short-cropped turf, pausing just long enough to count how many bikes there were.

'How many are there?' Adam asked, his deep voice startling her as she hadn't heard him following her across the grass.

'Five, all about the same size so, as Kate said, they're probably all around the same age. But where's the mine?' she demanded, turning in a complete circle. 'That end of the field is a complete jumble of hills and rocks, a bit like a mini-tor, but there's no ruined building with a tall chimney anywhere near here.'

'Well, if it isn't in this field then it must be in one near here, or they wouldn't have left their bikes,' Adam pointed out, and swiftly set off up the steep slope of the field towards the rough ground, his long legs making short work of the distance as he called back, 'I'll climb up there and see if there's anything visible over the next wall.'

'Here,' Mike said as he caught up with them. 'I brought torches and emergency packs, just in case.'

Maggie grabbed a torch and one of the bags, cross with herself that she'd completely forgotten about their equipment. She'd only jumped out of the cab to open the gate, then had got carried away with the hunt for evidence of the children.

She was hurrying to keep up with the men's far longer legs when she tripped over something near a stray gorse bush.

With a muttered imprecation she bent to see

what it was. Probably a broken branch from the last storm, or perhaps from hungry cattle taking advantage of the fact that gorse was one of the few native plants that grew and flowered right through the year. But it wasn't gorse. It was a piece of a weathered old sawn plank with a very fresh break at one end.

Maggie swung her torch around, wondering where the other piece had gone, and what a stray plank was doing up here in the first place. There certainly weren't any buildings that she could see, only the rocky formation in front of her, with the sprawl of dense gorse growing at its foot.

The beam caught a glimpse of the colour change on several branches that had been scuffed. One had been recently broken, as though some animal had tried to force a way into the bush.

'Not a very hospitable place to want to go,' she muttered as she peered through the density of the plant's prickly canopy, but there was definitely nothing there but a big dark shadow. The bushes were thick and vigorous but certainly weren't anywhere near big enough to hide five youngsters, let alone the ruin of an engine house for a mine.

'Can you see anything?' she called up to Mike and Adam, marvelling that she had no difficulty discerning which was which even though it was now nearly dark. Mike had the broader, more muscular shoulders, thanks to his regular attendance at a gym, but was several inches shorter than Adam's leaner, more naturally athletic body.

'Can't see anything that looks like a mine,' Mike called back down. 'We must have the wrong bikes for a different set of kids. Perhaps someone's been stealing them and stockpiling them up here, and is going to collect their stash at some time.'

'Where do you think we should look next?' Adam said as he leapt lightly from one rock to another until he landed almost at her feet, apparently unhampered by the second awkward bag of equipment he'd taken from Mike.

'I have absolutely no…' Maggie paused and turned her head from side to side. 'Shh! Did you hear that?'

'What?' Mike's footwear was clattering on the granite as he completed his descent to join them by the gorse bushes. 'I didn't hear anything.'

'There it is again,' Maggie insisted, and turned the beam of her torch towards the bush. 'It sounded almost as if a kitten's caught in that gorse.' •

Except it hadn't sounded exactly like that, because the noise was fainter and seemed much further away. Perhaps it was nothing more than the weak bleat of an early lamb in a nearby field. Perhaps...

'Perhaps it's the kids?' Mike suggested. 'Perhaps they're somewhere nearby and they can see the light from our torches and the flashes on our uniforms. Hey!' he shouted loudly, startling Maggie for a second. 'Is there anybody there?'

This time there was no mistaking the sound they heard because it was louder, as though someone was shouting with renewed energy now that there was someone listening.

'We're here!' called a distant childish voice

that definitely came from the middle of the gorse bush.

'But I looked there and couldn't see anything,' Maggie protested as Adam dropped to his knees beside her.

'Neither can I,' she heard him mutter, then stifle a curse when there was the unmistakable sound of ripping cloth as he tried to force a path through the sturdy stems and branches. 'Unless…Got it!' he exclaimed, and she and Mike heard the sound of splintering timber.

'What have you found?' Maggie demanded as she dropped to her knees behind him, grateful for the sturdy fabric of her uniform.

'I think it's the entrance to an adit,' Adam said tersely, then there was the sound of more splintering timber and a muttered, 'Ouch!'

'What's an adit?' Maggie demanded, even as she wondered what he'd done to hurt himself.

'It's a mining term for a horizontal—or nearly horizontal—shaft into a mine,' Mike explained distractedly as he took the broken pieces of wood Adam was passing back to him and stacked them aside. 'It was used for access or drainage, if I remember what my grandfather told me. He was a born and bred tin miner before the bottom dropped out of the international price of tin.'

'Yes! It *is* an adit!' Adam exclaimed over the screeching sound of rusty nails being dragged out of wood. 'It was obviously boarded up some time ago, either when the yield became uneconomic for the man hours needed to extract it or when the price of tin took that tumble. *I* certainly don't remember it ever being worked.'

'Is there anybody there?' called a young voice from the depths of the entrance Adam had uncovered.

'Yes!' Adam called back, his head stuck into the hole he'd enlarged by tearing the board away. 'I'm a doctor. *Who* are you and *where* are you?'

There was the sound of other voices far in the distance, but the one closest to them shouted back to his companions with a swift, 'Shut up, you lot! I won't be able to hear what they're saying with you making that racket!'

'One at a time, please,' Adam roared, and everything went quiet.

'There are five of us,' the young voice came again, and Maggie was impressed by how calm and controlled he sounded. If she'd been in the same situation…well, there was no chance of that. Her claustrophobia was a very good reason to steer clear of anything in the least bit mine-like. 'We're mostly all right,' continued the young voice, 'except Tel. He fell on the stope and then some rocks fell down and he's stuck under them… And there's wet on the floor under him, so we think he's bleeding, but we dropped our torch and the bulb broke so we can't see.'

'And who are you?' Adam asked, while Maggie itched to get the talking over and get those kids out of there. They'd been missing for over an hour now and…

'My name's Jem…Jeremiah Althorp, and my mum's… She used to work at the doctors surgery.'

'Kate!' Maggie exclaimed, suddenly remembering that the poor woman was waiting for news of her son.

Well, she thought as she speed-dialled the surgery, the number still in her phone from when her mother had been so ill, they might not know the full extent of everybody's injuries yet but, apart from an understandable tremor in his voice, Kate's son at least seemed to be relatively safe.

'Penhally Bay Surgery,' said the familiar reassuring voice of Hazel Furse. 'Can I help—?'

'Hazel, it's Maggie…Maggie Pascoe. Will you tell Kate that we've found the boys and that we've been talking to her son?'

'Oh, thank God!' Hazel exclaimed, then obviously pulled the receiver away from her ear to call across the reception area, 'They've found them!'

Maggie smiled when she heard the sudden hubbub and cheering at the other end, then Hazel was back on the line.

'Kate wants to know if you're coming straight back to Penhally with them…well, with Jem,' she added in a quieter voice.

'We won't be back for a bit, Hazel,' Maggie confessed. 'I wanted you all to know as soon as possible that we've located the lads, but we haven't got them out yet. I didn't want everyone to think that we were still looking for the right mine.'

'OK.' Hazel's tone was more subdued this time. 'So where are you and how difficult is it going to be to get them out? Are you going to need other emergency services to help? How many of the kids are injured and how badly?'

'We're on the road out of the valley, past the junction between Bridge Street and Dunheved Road, on the way to St Piran Hospital,' Maggie explained, trying to make the directions as simple and as clear as possible. 'There's a field on the left, just past a little lay-by, with the gate propped wide open. The ambulance is parked just inside the field facing towards some piles of rocks, with Dr Donnelly's car beside it. We're probably going to need a fire crew with ropes and ladders—oh, and another ambulance in case any of the lads need to travel on backboards. Apart from that, we won't really know until we can get close enough to them to see what we're dealing with.'

She shuddered at the thought of getting any closer to that mine entrance than she was now. Just the idea of going into that dark, dank opening was enough to make her claustrophobia send her pulse sky high and double her respiration rate.

'I'll pass all that on,' Hazel promised. 'Keep in touch, Maggie.'

'Will do,' she promised.

'Hey, Maggie, we need you here,' Mike called over his shoulder before she'd even cut the call.

'OK. Which set of equipment do you need?' she said as she squatted beside the prickly bushes that looked as if they were devouring the two men whole. All she could see of Mike was his legs and Adam was nothing more than two obviously male feet clad in a totally inappropriate pair of polished leather shoes.

Even as she watched, that pair of feet started to squirm backwards out of the gorse bush towards her and she could see that his smart suit trousers were already stained and snagged and probably damaged beyond any hope of repair.

'We're not ready for our boxes of tricks yet,'

Mike was saying as Adam straightened up and walked the two paces that put him right in front of her.

Pride made her stand her ground, even though the man's presence had a disastrous effect on her nervous system, and she forced herself to look him straight in the eye.

'Maggie...' he began, then it seemed as if he couldn't hold her gaze any more and he paused so long that she just knew she wasn't going to like what came next. 'Look, I know what I'm asking will be...very hard for you but... The thing is, the entrance to the mine is almost completely blocked by debris—loose rocks and suchlike—and neither Mike nor I will fit through it until it's been excavated.'

'Well, I've just been in contact with Hazel at the surgery,' she told him hastily, not liking the direction that her vivid imagination was taking her. 'She's going to let the emergency services know exactly where we are so they shouldn't be long. Then we'll have all the equipment and manpower we need to—'

'Maggie,' he interrupted gently. 'I managed to shine a torch far enough along the adit for Jem to be able to see it reflected off the walls, so he's absolutely certain that we're here. Didn't you hear him tell me that there's a puddle of blood under one of the lads…the one trapped by the rockfall? From what he said, I don't think that boy can afford to wait for anyone else to turn up because we don't know whether he's bleeding out, or heading for crush syndrome, or what. It's entirely probable that his only chance of staying alive is for one of us to go down there and take care of him. Mike and I are just too bulky to get through that gap, so that just leaves you.'

'*Me?* But I *can't*!' she squeaked as panic tightened its grip around her throat. 'Adam, you *know* I can't. Y-you know that I'm—'

'Maggie, stop! You're hyperventilating. Take a breath!' he ordered, his voice sharp even though it was barely above a whisper in the quiet of the Cornish countryside. He held both her shoulders in warm, firm hands, his thumbs stroking her soothingly through the sturdy fabric of her uniform and sending a shower of shivers through her body. 'You *can* do it.'

'*No!* I—'

'Shh!' he soothed. 'I know the whole idea freaks you out, but you've done it before. Remember?'

'Remember? Of *course* I remember!' she snapped. 'I didn't sleep properly for months after that nightmare of an afternoon. You *can't* ask me to go in there when you know how bad—'

'Maggie, I'm not asking you to do it for *me*,' he reminded her, with a little shake of her shoulders. 'I've got a bad feeling about that lad trapped by the rocks.'

That stopped her in her tracks.

She'd been part of the medical profession long enough to respect her colleagues' intuition about a situation. Often it flew in the face of logic, but it was uncanny how often it was right, so if Adam had a bad feeling about Tel's condition…

'How bad do you think it is?'

'Well, we all know that youngsters like to exaggerate the gorier things in life but, from what

Jem said, I'm almost certain that his friend's leg has been badly broken by the rocks, and you know as well as I do that he's likely to lose the leg altogether if he isn't released soon. But it's the blood loss that I'm most concerned about,' he stressed, knowing she would understand the significance of such a situation. 'There's far too much of it, if Jem's description is accurate, and I'm wondering if the bone was splintered by the impact and has done some major venous or arterial damage.'

'So you think there's a serious chance that he might be bleeding out?' she whispered, suddenly understanding that there *was* something worse than being asked to face one of her worst fears. Being claustrophobic and having to go underground was nothing compared with the prospect of bleeding to death trapped under a pile of rocks. Then there was the prospect of the youngster developing crush syndrome, which could be equally fatal when the pressure was finally removed.

For just a second, as she pictured herself

crawling through into that awful darkness, she was certain that she couldn't do it, but then she realised something more important. If she *didn't* do it, and the lad died, she would never be able to forgive herself. The fact that the young woman she'd tended under the underground train had survived and was slowly getting on with her life had been one of the few things that had made all the nightmares worthwhile.

'Adam, promise me you'll stay close,' she begged, the words already hovering in the chilly air between them before she'd realised she was going to say anything, her breath swirling around them like tortured wraiths.

'Of course I'll be here for you, Maggie. Like I was last time,' he promised, and she knew that whatever else had gone wrong between them, he wouldn't break his word to her.

'So,' she said, trying desperately to sound brisk but very conscious that her teeth were starting to chatter at the imminent prospect of climbing into the mine, 'how are we going to do this? What do you want me to do?'

'To put it at its most basic, you need to get in far enough to find out what's happened to those kids. Start with basic triage, the way you would with every callout. Find out how many are injured and how badly and prioritise how you need to deal with them.'

'Until I'm in there I'm not going to know how much kit I can take with me,' Maggie pointed out, concerned that she might not have the right equipment to hand when she reached the boys. 'A lot of our stuff is in portable boxes or bags because we often have to start work on a patient away from the ambulance. But if I'm the only one going in and I'm going to be climbing or…or squeezing through small spaces…' She swallowed hard, her imagination already far too vivid for peace of mind.

'Prioritise,' he repeated firmly. 'Most of all, we need to find out what we can do for the one who's trapped. See if it's possible to release him or will he just have to be stabilised as best you can until we can get some muscle or some serious machinery in there to free him and get him out?'

'And in my spare time…' she said ironically.

Adam gave a short huff of laughter and she caught a brief glimpse of that grin again. 'In your spare time, Maggie, you could keep up a running commentary so that I can be certain that you're all right.'

Then there was no more time to delay, not if that lad was bleeding as badly as Jem thought he was.

'Coming through,' she said to Mike as she threaded her way through the gorse. It wasn't until she was almost at the dreaded black hole, framed now by the last remnants of the broken and rotted boards, that she realised that he'd spent his time while she and Adam had been speaking in ripping the jagged timber away so that she could see better to climb over the rubble blocking the entrance to the adit.

'Maggie, just think about this for a minute,' her colleague cautioned quietly when she reached out a shaky hand towards the rough rocks. 'The first rule of rescue work is never to endanger yourself, and this definitely comes under the heading of—'

'Don't, Mike,' she said with a single shake of her head, knowing he was right but also knowing that she had to be able to live with her own conscience.

'Maggie, I know those lads need help,' he tried again, holding onto her arm to prevent her moving any further forward. 'But you could lose your job for going in there without the proper—'

'Mike, you know how much I love my job, but I don't think I'd *want* it any more if I let any of those kids die when I could have done something to prevent it,' she said with an unexpected feeling of determination. 'I'm not going in there because I want to but because I have to, and the best way you can help is to stand by with the bags of equipment ready to pass me the supplies I need when I get in there.'

'Ready to go, Maggie?' Adam prompted from close behind her, but she'd already known he was there, silently supporting her as she argued her case. 'Take my torch,' he offered as she nodded and took a deep breath. 'It's not as heavy-duty as yours but I think it gives out just as much light.'

'Thank you,' she whispered, gazing back for one last second into those shadowy midnight-blue eyes. Then she forced herself to begin squeezing though the awkward opening at the top of the rockfall that was blocking most of the entrance and preventing the two men from taking her place in there.

Once inside, she put her hand back out again to be passed her emergency pack of basic equipment and then it was time to crawl into the blackness.

For several paces she concentrated so hard on controlling her breathing and putting one hand and knee in front of the other that she didn't pay much attention to her surroundings. It wasn't until the heel of the hand holding Adam's torch landed on a painfully sharp piece of rock that she paused for a second to rub it and caught sight of something that surprised her.

'Hey! Adam…Mike, it's not just a tiny tunnel in here!' she exclaimed with a definite feeling of relief. 'I can actually stand up in it once I'm past the rockfall at the entrance!' She suited her actions to her words and swung briefly back towards the entrance, suddenly uneasily aware that if she hadn't been looking directly at it, she wouldn't have known where it was. It was now so dark outside that the only light visible was from her own torch and the one held by whoever was immediately outside the entrance. The rough pile of rocks that were blocking the entrance made that part of the mine look no different from any other part.

'Can you pass the other equipment packs through?' she suggested. 'It looks as if there'll be plenty of room, and I might be able to carry them all the way to where the boys are. That would save time.'

'Stick to plan A,' Adam advised, his voice sounding strangely hollow as it echoed around her. 'Just take your lightweight emergency pack with the basics. It's better to locate the boys and find out what you're dealing with before you start loading yourself down unnecessarily. Then you can decide what's the best way to proceed. You can always come back for more.'

'Anyway,' Mike's disembodied voice added his twopenn'orth, 'while you're doing that, we're going to be clearing as much of this rock away as we can, so we can get in there to help.'

'OK,' she agreed, and turned back to the tunnel with a shudder.

Adam was right, of course, but, then, he'd already worked as an emergency specialist in a big London hospital and had gained enough experience to be able to take over teaching the course she'd gone up to attend when the original lecturer had been taken ill.

She could feel herself smiling when she remembered her delight at seeing him walk into that lecture room. It had been so many years since the last time she'd seen him but one look at that lean athletic body and the familiar planes and angles of his face had been enough to know this really was the man who'd been haunting her dreams since she'd been an impressionable teenager.

The answering flash of recognition in those beautiful deep blue eyes had made her grateful that she'd been sitting down. The last thing she'd needed in front of a roomful of colleagues had been to make a fool of herself by falling at his feet.

'Ouch!' she yelped as her head hit an obstruction and she dropped to one knee to give it a rub.

'What's the matter?' Adam demanded instantly. 'Maggie, are you all right?'

'I hit my head on something,' she complained crossly, and shone her torch upwards to see if she could find the obstruction. Was the roof dropping that much lower already? How long would it be before she was reduced to crawling again?

When she saw the dangling balk of wood thicker than her thigh that should have been supporting the ceiling, she wished that she hadn't bothered looking.

Suddenly she was overwhelmingly conscious of just how many tons of rock were sitting just inches above her head, and she found herself fighting to draw in enough air.

'Maggie?' Adam called. 'You're supposed to be talking to me, remember?'

She was so panic-stricken that she could barely remember her own name, and as for breathing…

'Maggie!' he called again with worry clear in his voice. 'Can you hear me? Are you all right?'

'Yes,' she croaked, and had to clear her throat, but his concern had helped her to regain control. 'Yes, Adam, I can hear you.'

'What's happening, then? I heard you cry out. Did you injure yourself?'

'I hit my head,' she said shortly, giving the spot another rub once she'd made certain that she hadn't done enough damage to make it bleed.

'What did you hit your head on? Does the roof slope down that sharply?'

'It wasn't the roof,' she said, forcing herself to say the words without thinking about the significance of them. 'It was one of those wood thingies that holds up the roof. It's come off the upright one and was hanging down low enough for me to walk into it.'

She thought she heard Adam swear but his voice when he spoke was calmness personified.

'Mike says he thinks those are called sprags or gibs, depending where you are,' he told her…as if she was interested in the name of the thing she'd hit. All she was worried about was whether the fact that only one end of the wretched thing was where it was supposed to be meant that the roof wasn't being held up properly.

No! She wasn't going to think about that. There were five young lads waiting for her to get to them…relying on her to sort out their injuries before they could be helped out of the mine.

'Jem!' she called when her next few careful steps brought her to an apparent choice of directions. 'Where are you?'

'I'm here, straight ahead of you,' said a boyish voice, so unexpectedly close that he made her jump. His face was nearly at floor level a dozen or more yards ahead of her and, apart from smears of dirt, was almost totally devoid of colour when she caught him in her torchlight.

There was no mistaking that he was Kate's

son, she thought with an internal grin, not with that dark hair and brown eyes set off in that bone structure.

She began to hurry forward, wondering if he was lying there because he was injured or trapped, but he quickly called out, 'Don't come too close. I'm on the top of a stope.'

Maggie paused uncertainly, her need to check that he wasn't too badly injured barely kept in check. 'What's a stope?' she asked.

'It's where the miners were following a vein of ore and the excavation leaves steps in the rock. I found out all about it on the internet for a school project.'

'Steps? But that's great!' Maggie exclaimed as she started forward again, more cautiously this time. 'That'll make it much easier to get you all out.' Much easier than if the boys had fallen down a narrow shaft, for example.

'No. You don't understand,' he said urgently, clearly wanting her to stop. 'They're not solid steps. They're all broken and crumbly in places. That's how Tel fell.'

'Tell me what happened,' she prompted as she slowly crept forward on hands and knees again, to peer over the edge and down the precipitous stepped slope. Was this the moment when she was going to discover that she had a fear of heights, too?

'He didn't fall very far but some rocks came down and landed on him. The rest of us climbed down the rest of the way to help him get out again,' he continued, the words pouring out in an urgent, jerky stream. 'We were trying to move the rocks and Chris got hurt, then we dropped the torch and the bulb broke and we couldn't see what we were doing any more, and then I said I'd come back up to get help but I couldn't get up this last bit because I'm not tall enough, and the signal was too weak on my mobile so I couldn't tell Mum where we were. Then it got too dark and I didn't dare climb down again, so I was stuck here till you came.'

'So, where is Tel now?' she asked when she'd finally eased forward enough to see down the stope and beyond, shining the torchlight against the jumble of rocks at the bottom of the jagged steps and shuddering at the size of them. If something that size had landed on one of the boys, there would be little likelihood that they'd survived. 'Your message said that one of the boys is bleeding. That's Tel, is it?'

'Uh-huh.' He nodded. 'And he's unconscious.'

'Can you see where the blood is coming from? His head, his body…?'

'I think it's his leg,' he said with a frown, 'but there's a load of rocks in the way so I can't see properly. And I can't move them either—they're too heavy.'

'Well, it won't be too long before we can get some big strong men down here to get them shifted,' she reassured him, even as her fears about crush syndrome increased, then took a deep breath to bolster herself for what she knew she had to do next. It might still be within the so-called golden hour for his young friend and she needed to start minimising the trauma he'd suffered as soon as possible.

'Jem, I need you to help me. I need you to

show me how to get down the…the stope…to have a look at Tel.'

'But…but you're a *girl*,' he said, screwing up his face in disbelief, and Maggie made a mental note to have a word with Kate about her son's gender stereotyping once this was all over.

'Yes, I am, but I'm a girl who used to do climbing ropes and gymnastics at school, and climbing over the rocks under the lighthouse every holiday.'

He still didn't look as if he believed her and she was aware of his reluctance as he guided her through every shaky step she took as she lowered herself feet first over that first enormous drop then edged backwards down the rest of the ragged steps of the stope.

'They're behind here,' he said, hurrying forward towards another pile of rock that looked as if it had been there for centuries…the pile of boulders she'd been looking at from the top just a few minutes ago looking even more enormous now she was close to them. 'Tel fell down the last bit of the stope, then some of the rocks started to fall and he tried to get out of the way so he was running into this other tunnel, but there were too many rocks coming and they were falling too fast and he couldn't get out of the way in time and they hit him and knocked him down. Some of them landed on him.'

He started climbing round the edge of the enormous pile of loose rocks and she suddenly caught sight of another tunnel entrance that had been almost completely hidden from view. Her heart began to pound with renewed panic when she saw how small it was. It was narrower than the one at the top of the stope. Much narrower and not nearly as high.

I can't do this, said a panicky voice in her head, and her feet froze to the dank, gritty ground. *I won't be able to breathe in there; there won't be enough air, especially if I have to share it with all these other people.*

CHAPTER THREE

'MAGGIE?' Jem turned back to her before he joined his friends in the second tunnel, his eyes very dark in the gloom, and she had the feeling that he was deliberately keeping his voice low so that they couldn't hear him. 'I'm...I'm really glad you came to find us. It was scary being down here all by ourselves...without any light.'

Suddenly she was ashamed of herself. She had a light—Adam's torch—and the certainty that, by now, there were probably dozens of people arriving in the field around the entrance to the adit, and all of them would be working out the best way to get them all out safely. All she had to do was the job she was trained for...to assess the injuries this group of lads had sustained and to stabilise them as far as possible until further help arrived.

The fact that she would rather be a million miles away was *her* problem, not theirs, and she couldn't let it affect the care she gave them.

'Hey! It's a girl! I thought you said it was someone coming to help us!' said another disgusted young voice, dragging her back to the whole reason she was putting herself through this misery. Maggie added a fresh mental note to suggest a visit to their school to tell them all about the wide variety of job possibilities for *girls* in the twenty-first century.

'I'm a paramedic,' she corrected him gently as she caught him in the bright light of Adam's torch, 'and I need to know what injuries you've all got.'

'Dwayne, me and Jonno haven't got any injuries,' Jem said swiftly, acting as spokesman. 'Chris got his hand hurt when it was squished by a rock, but Tel's the one who's hurt the worst.'

While he'd been giving her the details, he'd

been pointing to the other lads and she quickly threaded her way through rocks and boys to bend over the silent youngster trapped by the fallen rocks.

'Is he still alive?' Jem demanded uncertainly as her gloved fingertips probed for the carotid artery in the dust-caked neck. 'I thought he was when I tried before, but I wasn't sure I was looking in the right place...'

'Yes. He's still alive. His heart's still beating, Jem,' she confirmed, remembering to smile her reassurance in spite of the fact that the pulse was weaker and faster than she would have wanted. And it was hardly any wonder that his breathing was laboured with that amount of rock inhibiting the movement of his ribcage.

He was obviously going to need fluids and a far more detailed examination, but there just wasn't room in these cramped conditions, not with so many heads leaning over her shoulder to see what she was doing.

There was only one alternative so, much as

everything in her was telling her that she needed to attend to the most seriously injured child first, she beckoned forward the one that Jem had called Chris.

'Come here, Chris. Show me your hand,' she said, a quick flash of her torch across his face reassuring her that his pupils were equal and reactive. The fact that it had also revealed the telltale tracks of hastily smeared tears was something she wouldn't be mentioning to anyone.

'You won't hurt it, will you?' he asked, as he held his other hand protectively over it.

'I promise I'll be gentle, but I need to know what sort of injury you've got or I can't do anything for it,' she explained, and hid a smile at his reluctant acquiescence.

'Ouch!' she said in sympathy when she saw his bruised and swollen hand. 'It looks like the rock caught you right on the back of your hand. Can you move your fingers?'

'Don't know. It'll hurt too much if I do.'

'Can you try…just once?' she appealed, then realised she might be missing out on the youngster's need for drama. 'I need to see if your tendons, muscles and nerves are still working.'

His eyes widened, so obviously she'd made her request seem important enough to impress. 'OK,' he said grudgingly. 'But I only have to do it once, right?'

'Right,' she agreed, then held her hand out flat towards him. 'And if you put your hand on mine, you'll only need to move your fingers a tiny bit and I'll be able to feel it.'

He gingerly lowered the purple swollen mass onto her palm, drawing a sharp hiss of breath in through his teeth at one point before looking up at her.

'Ready?' she prompted gently, wishing there was such a thing as a miniature portable X-ray to help her make a diagnosis. As it was, she didn't even dare to give him any analgesia in case his only way out was to climb up that deadly stope.

'Brilliant!' she praised when she felt him carefully move each finger one by one, his face screwed up against the pain. 'I felt each of them move,' she confirmed, and when she saw the relief on his face she was glad he didn't know that it wasn't the whole story. His nerves and tendons might have escaped major injury, but she'd definitely detected the crepitation of at least one broken metacarpal and wouldn't be surprised if there was more than one.

'Right, Chris,' she said briskly as she reached into her backpack and drew out a folded square of fabric. She was all too aware that time was passing and she still had to see Tel. 'I need to immobilise your hand so that you don't do it any further damage.'

Years of practice meant that it took mere seconds to fashion an impressive sling to support his hand up against his opposite shoulder. Not knowing how seriously Tel was hurt meant she daren't take the time to apply a splint.

'Is that more comfortable?' she asked, and received a grateful nod. 'Well, if your friends give you a hand, do you think you could climb out over the pile in front of the tunnel to give me a bit more room? I need to be able to get closer to Tel to see what the rocks have done to him. Has he been talking to you at all since they fell on him?'

'He's moaned a couple of times,' said one of the lads.

'And Jem felt his neck a couple of times to see if he's still got a pulse, and you said he has, so that means he's still alive, doesn't it?' said another, as the two of them scrambled over the rocks to get out of the confining space, almost forgetting to take their injured friend with them in their eagerness. At the last moment, each of them held out a hand towards Chris and took his arms to help him to keep his balance without disturbing his injured hand.

Once they were out of the confining space, all three of them were obviously keen to move away from it and Maggie knew how they felt. She wasn't in the least bit keen to stay in there either, even though she knew she had to.

For just a second she flicked the torch beam out of the narrow tunnel and up the stope towards the darker shadow of the adit at the top…the tunnel that led to the opening into the outside world where Adam was waiting to hear what was happening… And the one thing she wanted most in the whole world was to get out of there as fast as she could and throw herself into his arms.

'And that just shows how being down here is messing with your mind,' she muttered under her breath. Adam may have been her hero when she'd been looking up to the handsome senior at school and weaving for-ever-after fantasies around him, but he'd de-veloped feet of clay since. He certainly wasn't a person she could trust with her heart, but she didn't have any option but to trust him with her safety.

'Stay close, lads,' Maggie warned as the three of them disappeared out of sight behind the pile of rocks. This was no time for losing concentra-tion, she reminded herself sternly as she banished Adam from her mind. She had an injured child who was relying on her to stabilise him, ready for the moment when the rescue team arrived. 'I wouldn't be able to cope if there were any more injuries, so don't go wandering off.'

She turned the torch back to focus on the last able-bodied youngster. 'Jem, it's your turn to climb out of here,' she said encouragingly, but he shook his head, the pale face topped with that dark shock of hair set in determination.

'I'm staying in here with Tel,' he said stubbornly. 'He knows me…and anyway you might need my help.'

Maggie was torn between wanting to hug the boy for providing her with company in this awful place and fearing that she would let herself down in front of him with a major panic attack.

'Well, a second pair of hands could come in useful so we'd better see what we can do for him,' she said, and bent to clear a small space among the smaller rocks so she could kneel as close as possible to the unconscious youngster, then dipped her shoulder and slid the all-important rucksack to the ground.

'Is his heart still beating?' Jem demanded, clearly concerned as her gloved fingertips probed once more for the too-rapid beat of his carotid artery. 'I was checking it before I climbed up the stope but then the torch got bust and it got dark outside so there wasn't any light coming in any more, and the others didn't know where to look…'

Maggie didn't need to be reminded just how dark it was or how far away the entrance was from where she was kneeling, and the only way to banish it from her mind was to concentrate on the messages her fingers were sending her mind and her conversation with this bright youngster.

'Yes. His heart's still beating, Jem,' she said, remembering once more to smile her reassurance.

As for the dark pool seeping out from under him, all she could hope was that there was a fair amount of water mixed in with it. If it was only blood, the youngster must be close to critical with that amount of loss.

Either way, it was imperative that she put a collar on him to immobilise his neck. If the lad woke up and tried to move, it could be too late to protect his spinal cord. Then she needed to get some replacement fluids into him to give his heart some volume to pump around.

'Right, Jem, if you want to make yourself useful, can you hold the torch for me, please? If you point it this way, I'll be able to find what I need to protect his neck. Then I want to put up a drip to get some fluids flowing into him,' she explained as she unzipped the relevant compartment and tilted it towards the light to find and pull out a cervical collar, then locate a giving set and a unit of saline. 'That way, everything will be ready to give him any drugs he needs.'

'It's a good job he doesn't know you're going to stick a needle in him,' Jem commented with glee as he watched her swab his friend's grubby arm then slide the needle in, hitting the vein she was looking for first time in spite of the limited lighting. 'Tel doesn't like needles. He says just looking at them makes him feel sick, but I think he's scared they'll hurt.'

'You don't mind them, though?' she asked, quite taken with this self-possessed young boy. He was certainly far braver than she would have been in a similar situation.

'Nah,' he said dismissively. 'I watch all the medical programmes on TV…not just the fiction ones but the real ones in real hospitals, too…so needles don't bother me. Do you want me to hold that bag of water up, too?'

'That would be great,' she confirmed. 'And it's not just water in there—it's called saline because it's had a small amount of salt added to it.'

'Salt?' he exclaimed. 'Why?'

'Because our bodies don't work very well if they don't have the right amount of salt. It causes problems if we eat too much of it, but we also need to have it replaced if we've been losing fluids.'

'Otherwise you can get cramp?' he suggested brightly. 'Like I did after last sports day when we were running and got very sweaty when the sun was so hot?'

'Exactly!' Maggie exclaimed, keeping up the

conversation while her fingers covered as much of Tel's body as she could reach, searching for any obvious injuries. 'It's very similar to that.'

She paused to sit back on her heels, delighted to confirm that, apart from a large goose egg on the back of his head, her young patient didn't have any obvious cranial injuries. As far as she could tell, the swelling was nothing more than a surface haematoma. If he was lucky, he would wake up with nothing worse than a mammoth headache and suffer from the effects of concussion.

But none of that was as daunting as the enormity of the next task she faced before she could complete her survey of Tel's injuries. There were an awful lot of rocks that had spilled into the mouth of this cramped tunnel and she was going to have to find out exactly how many of them were pressing down on him to know what the likelihood was that he was in danger of developing crush syndrome. Only then would she dare remove the pressure from Tel's ribs and legs.

And none of it was going to happen if she just sat here looking at it, she prompted herself. It seemed highly unlikely that Adam and Mike would have cleared enough from the heap by the entrance yet to be joining her any time soon. So that meant it was her job.

'Jem, are you OK, holding that for a while?' she asked with a shiver as the dank cold seemed to seep into her bones, suddenly realising that having to shift those rocks might have a good side to it. At least the physical activity would help to warm her up. 'I need to try to shift a few of these rocks so I can see where this blood's coming from.'

'Otherwise all the...the *saline* will be leaking out again?' he suggested cheerfully.

'You've got it.' She smiled across at him, strangely proud that he'd remembered the word she'd taught him, and wondered if that was what life would be like if she had a son of her own.

Unfortunately, the image that flashed into her head was a child with Adam's dark sapphire eyes and mischievous grin, and she knew *that* prospect was a complete impossibility. It wouldn't matter how much she still loved him or how attracted he was to her, she would never break her own code of ethics and sleep with a married man...not unless he was married to *her*. And that could certainly never be the case with Adam because he was already married to the elegant long-limbed beauty with the curtain of blonde hair that she'd seen in the wedding photo beside his bed.

She gave herself a shake and a silent talking-to for wasting time with painful memories and pointless daydreaming, and reached for the first rock, surprised as ever how very heavy even a relatively small piece of granite could be.

It was fairly easy to shift the smaller stuff that had rolled away from the pile and she quickly cleared a space right down one side of Tel's body. Unfortunately, that only told her that, battered and bruised as it was, *that* leg wasn't the one that was bleeding. It did, however, tell her that the position of the rocks made crush syndrome unlikely, so that was one good point at least.

'We're getting there,' she reassured Jem, conscious that he was following her every move as she reached for one of the larger rocks poised atop the whole heap piled against the wall of the tunnel.

'Careful!' Jem called, as she set off a minor avalanche as soon as she gave the rock a tug.

It seemed to take for ever before everything stopped moving and even then there were odd creaks and groans as the debris settled into its new position.

'What happened?'

'Are you guys all right?' demanded an instant chorus at the opening to the tunnel.

'We're OK,' Maggie said when she could draw breath in the dusty atmosphere, knowing they needed reassurance from the only adult in the vicinity. For several very long seconds all she'd been able to imagine was that she was about to be buried alive, and her throat had closed up completely.

'Jem, can you shine the torch over a bit?' she asked, hoping they couldn't hear how much her voice was trembling with gratitude that it had only been a rearrangement of the rocks that were already there and not a fresh fall. It was bad enough that she was down here, having to cope with a lifelong phobia—at least she had the mental reassurance that at any time she had the option of climbing back up the stope to get out. She definitely couldn't cope if she knew she was trapped down there, like Tel.

Her thoughts suddenly flashed back to that awful afternoon in the London underground when a man and a woman had fallen—or jumped—off the platform into the path of an approaching train.

Maggie had been certain that she wouldn't be able to deal with squeezing herself between the rails, with the dark smelly bulk of the train just inches above her head, while she tried to staunch the bleeding from the girl's partially severed arm. Only the fact that Adam had been there, calmly talking her through the whole ordeal, had kept her rational enough to do what had to be done.

Even having Adam with her wouldn't be able to keep her sane if she were trapped deep underground, so she would just have to get moving and get everyone out as fast as possible. And that meant starting all over again, laboriously clearing the little stones and rocks first, and then tackling the bigger ones until she could find and deal with the injury that was causing Tel's blood loss.

'None of the rocks hit you, did they, Jem?' she asked as she settled into a rhythm for grabbing the next rock and stacking it out of the way against the opposite wall of the tunnel.

'Nah!' he said dismissively. 'But I bet you got a few bruises on your legs. I saw some of them hit you. Are you all right?'

'I might be all the colours of the rainbow in a day or two,' she conceded, her breathing becoming slightly laboured with the repetitive effort. *Or was it the start of air hunger?* a little voice inside her head suggested insidiously. *Were they running out of air? Would all of them pass out because there wasn't enough oxygen to support…?*

Enough! she admonished herself silently. Adam and Mike were widening the entrance. There was plenty of air coming in. Concentrate on talking to Jem and moving the rocks to find out where his friend was injured. There wasn't time to think about anything else. 'But bruises are quick to heal,' she continued lightly, 'especially if you're reasonably healthy, so it's not really a problem unless it causes a major bleed.'

'Anyway, you're a girl, so you wouldn't be a haemophiliac, would you?' he said knowledgeably. 'We learned about haemophilia when we had a boy in our class who had to be careful that he didn't fall in the playground and Miss Venning was telling us about the Russian king whose children had it. They got it from our Queen Victoria, didn't they?'

'She was a carrier of the condition, I believe,' Maggie agreed.

'It always seems odd,' he said thoughtfully, 'that a woman can give her children a blood disease or…or colour-blindness, without knowing about it because it doesn't affect her.' He switched the bag of saline from one hand to the other, and the way he was bracing it against the wall told her that although his arms were obviously beginning to ache, he wouldn't be complaining. 'And eye colour is another thing,' he went on. 'There's someone in Mr Tolliver's class who's got one blue eye and one brown one. It's really cool. Mine are just brown, 'cos both my mum and dad's were.'

'Well, mine turned out a mixture of green and brown,' Maggie volunteered, and found herself wondering pointlessly what colour her children's eyes would have been if she'd married Adam. She knew that brown was dominant over blue, but would her hazel eye colour have been dominant over his dark sapphire blue or vice versa?

'Maggie...?' called a voice in the distance, and even though it was distorted by echoes, her heart recognised it and gave an extra thump.

Adam!

Had he and Mike cleared enough of the entrance already?

Was he on his way down to join her?

Her knees complained when she straightened up enough from her cramped position to call over the mound of rocks that still blocked the entrance to the tunnel.

'Adam,' she called back, suddenly guiltily remembering that she'd been going to keep up a running commentary for those left outside. 'We're OK.' Well, that was true up to a point, and it would be even better once she'd finished shifting these rocks and could see where Tel's injury was.

'How many injured?' he shouted—at least, that's what it sounded like when she'd unscrambled the echoes.

'Two,' she yelled back, horrified to find that her exertions had left her panting. She'd honestly thought she was fitter than this. She certainly wouldn't allow herself to think about her disappointment that he obviously wasn't on his way down to help her yet. 'One minor and one major.'

Suddenly, the fact that he was a married man didn't matter. She was just so grateful that he was there and that he was checking up on her safety that, had he been close enough, she could have thrown herself into his arms without a qualm.

'Coming out?' he asked, and she had to take a guess at the first part of the question.

For a second she contemplated the order that things should be done and balanced them against what was possible. She had another bag of saline, but the rate that the first one was emptying meant that it wouldn't last very long. Then there were the three boys waiting at the bottom of the stope. She certainly couldn't guarantee how much longer their patience would last, and if they tried to climb that treacherous stepped wall without adequate lighting, there was no knowing how many injuries they could end up with.

'Five minutes,' she shouted back, and from the muted cheer from the other lads she knew they had been following the exchange.

'You're never going to be able to shift all those rocks in five minutes,' Jem said a minute later, after she'd resumed her efforts with the slowly diminishing heap. 'And we can't just go and leave Tel down here. We *can't!*'

'Jem, I've got no intention of leaving Tel

down here,' she said quickly, stricken that he'd been left thinking that it was even a possibility. 'I'm hoping that I can clear enough rocks away to find out where the blood's coming from, and stop it. But I'm going to need to fetch some more saline and I'll need to bring a backboard down to put him on before he can be carried out, so I may as well get the rest of you out of here at the same time. Your parents are probably all waiting up at the mouth of the stope, terrified that they're never going to see you again.'

'Oh.' He subsided, and she saw his grubby forehead pleat in a thoughtful frown before she turned to choose the next rock to pit her puny muscles against. There was just one last big one that, thankfully, had landed between Tel's legs and had prevented several others from hitting him, but if she tried to move it, she risked setting off another avalanche. But if she could just remove some of the smaller ones and slide her hand in underneath, she might be able to discover whether the bleeding was in the upper or lower half of his leg.

It was closer to ten minutes before she'd achieved her aim and was able to explore the wet proof that the injury was in his lower leg before she realised that her gloves had been totally shredded by her exertions with the rough granite.

'Damn,' she muttered under her breath as she quickly pulled her hand out and stared at the evidence. Hopefully, Tel was too young to have any of the more serious blood-borne infections, because the blood coating her scratched and grazed fingers couldn't help but find plenty of ways into her own system.

Well, she certainly didn't have any water to spare to wash her hand off and there wasn't enough time or sterile wipes to do the job, or light enough to see how thorough a job she was doing, so she was just going to have to get on with it and hope for the best.

The fact that his foot was facing in the wrong direction told her that there had been some sort of serious damage to his leg, but until she completed her examination she wouldn't know whether it was a dislocation of one of the joints—with all the concomitant dangers of impingement of nerve or blood supply, a femoral break—with the danger of life-threatening blood loss, or damage to the tibia or fibula, or both.

She gritted her teeth and slid her hand back between the rocks, only to have to stifle another groan when she felt the obvious evidence that both Tel's tibia and fibula *were* broken. At least she could feel that he still had circulation in his foot and his reflexes appeared to be intact. Added to that, it seemed as if the bones were only marginally displaced, so perhaps the bleeding was from the gash on his skin where the rock had impacted to cause the fractures.

Still, his pulse had become steadier and stronger since she'd set up the IV, and with the rocks moved away from his chest his breathing wasn't being impeded any more, although there were definitely several cracked ribs to worry about when the time came to move him onto a stretcher. The last thing he needed was a punctured lung or, worse yet, damage to his heart.

For now, she'd done everything she could

until he either regained consciousness or the rescue team was able to join her down here to shift the rest of the rocks.

'Right, Jem,' she said as she straightened up from checking the IV site and showed him how the new pile of rocks she'd been building as she took them away from Tel could just about be used as a temporary support for the second bag of saline. 'It's time I got the rest of you out of here. Let's go.'

'I'm not going,' Jem announced with a stubborn expression on his pale face.

'Jem…' she began, but he shook his head.

'I'm not leaving Tel down here all by himself,' he said firmly. 'If he wakes up and there's no one here…no one to tell him that someone knows he's here and that they're just making the hole bigger so they can get him out…'

Maggie shuddered at the very thought of waking up to utter darkness with the weight of millions of tons of granite looming over her head, but she could see that there was going to be no changing the youngster's mind.

It took her a moment to rearrange her thoughts. She wouldn't dream of leaving Jem in the dark. It had been bad enough thinking about leaving Tel without any light, and he was unconscious.

'Ok, if that's what you want…' She took the torch Adam had lent her and propped it carefully on the heap of stones still partially blocking the entrance to the tunnel. If she positioned it just right, it should light their way up the stope while she and the other three boys were climbing. 'I'm leaving the torch here with you,' she said, only just remembering boyish pride in time to add hastily, 'It would get in my way while I'm helping Chris keep his balance—he can't use his hand to hold on to anything. I'll need you to be in charge of it to show me where I'm going on the way back down, too.'

'I can do that,' he said, his voice far steadier than her own as he moved forward a little bit so that he could keep an eye on the torch and the drip at the same time. 'Just tell me where you want me to point it.'

'I will,' she agreed, before clambering over the rocks to join the lads waiting impatiently at the foot of the stope.

'Maggie...?' Adam's voice echoed, the strange reverberations making it seem as if it was coming from several directions at once.

'Coming,' she called back, and gestured for the two able-bodied lads to start climbing. 'Don't go too fast,' she cautioned when they began to race up the potentially deadly wall. 'I might need your help with Chris.'

'I'll be all right,' the injured youngster said bravely, but the expression on his face as he craned his neck to eye the climb he was going to have to make said something else entirely.

'You probably will, but I'm worried about your hand. I don't want you to do it any further damage before we can get an X-ray taken,' she explained as she steadied his elbow for the first, relatively easy step.

By the time they reached the last climb—the step that nearly came up to her shoulder—Maggie was shaking with exhaustion and desperately glad that Jonno and Dwayne were there to help her get Chris up the last hurdle between them and freedom.

'Don't run on ahead,' she warned when they were all on relatively level ground again. 'There's a big piece of wood hanging down from the roof and I don't want any of you to knock yourselves out.'

She might as well have saved her breath as far as Dwayne and Jonno were concerned. They could see light at the end of the tunnel…literally…and all they could think of was to get there as soon as possible.

'Hang on, lads. One at a time,' said a firm masculine voice up ahead as she matched the slower pace that Chris was forced to adopt so that he didn't jar his injured hand. 'It's taken us a long time to get this entrance shored up. We don't want you spoiling all our good work in your rush to get out.'

'Your turn, Chris,' she said when they finally reached the mouth of the adit, surprised that so little seemed to have been achieved in the time she'd been down below with the boys. She'd been expecting to see the entrance nearly clear by now, with equipment being readied for getting Tel out. All that seemed to have been achieved was that the gorse bushes had been cleared away and a series of steel props had been set up to hold fresh pieces of timber up against the roof of the entrance.

'Be careful of his hand,' she called to the unseen helpers outside. 'I've put a sling on him but he's going to need X-rays of those metacarpals.'

'Any more?' asked the same deep voice, and she could see the silhouette of a head wearing a safety helmet against the bright lights that had been set up outside.

'Just me this time,' she said as she began to climb, only remembering as it caught against the roughness of the hewn rocks that she hadn't been wearing her emergency pack when she'd come the other way—it had been passed through to her once she'd climbed through the hole.

It seemed as though a forest of hands was

reaching towards her to help her to her feet and even though the lights were bright enough to sear her eyes after the pitch black of the mine, the first face she focused on was Adam's.

'Well done,' she saw him say, although the sound of his praise was completely lost under the cacophony of a generator and voices that surrounded her, the area apparently filled with people in bulky, high-visibility gear.

She straightened up and filled her lungs with sweet, fresh air, relishing the ever-present tang of salt and wondering how she was ever going to be able to force herself do go back down that dank hole again.

CHAPTER FOUR

'No!'

One piercing shriek cut through everything else, silencing everything other than the steady all-pervading throb of the generator.

'Where's my son?' the shrill voice demanded. 'What's happened to my boy?'

'Kate…' someone said, and Maggie blinked. Was that dishevelled figure really Kate Althorp?

As Maggie watched, the normally smart former practice manager flung aside the restraining hand that Nick Tremayne tried to put around her shoulders and pushed her way through the knot of helmeted rescuers at the entrance to the adit towards Maggie.

'What have you done with my son?' she

demanded, glaring up at Maggie where she still stood on the heap of rocks. 'They said there were only two boys hurt and—'

'Kate,' Nick began again, having caught up with her, and Maggie saw him wrap a supporting arm around her shoulders. 'Take it easy. Give the girl a chance to catch her breath.'

'What do you mean, give her a chance to catch her breath?' Kate said, rounding on him furiously. 'I want to know why she hasn't brought my son up with the others. Is he the one that fell? Is he the one that's badly injured? Nick, you *know* what it was like when I lost James. You were there with me. I can't lose Jem, too. I couldn't *bear* it...'

'Kate!' Maggie called over her tirade, easily able to empathise with her terror. 'Jem *isn't* hurt.'

'He's not...' Relief warred with incomprehension, but it was anger that won. 'If he's *not* hurt, *why* didn't you bring him up with the others?' she demanded furiously. 'Why did you leave *my* son down there?'

'Because he refused to come up,' Maggie said, knowing that the simple truth would give Kate pause. She reached out a hand towards the tormented woman, even though she was too far away for any physical contact. 'Kate, Jem is the most amazing young lad I've ever met, and you should be proud of him. He didn't want to leave his friend in case he woke up alone in the dark.'

'Oh, God, help me…' Kate sobbed, but when she turned towards Nick, obviously needing his support, he wasn't there.

'That's the most ridiculous thing I've ever heard,' he said, striding towards Maggie with an accusing glare. 'He's only eight years old, for heaven's sake! I'm going down to bring him up,' he announced, intent on pushing his way through the rescue team already working systematically to clear the mouth of the adit.

'I can't let you do that, Dr Tremayne,' said a man with a similar air of authority, but *he* was wearing the appropriate safety gear and in spite of his youth was obviously the leader of the rescue team.

'You can't stop me,' the GP said belligerently, trying to stare him down. 'I've been on more rescue missions than you've had hot dinners.'

'That may well be true, Doctor,' the younger man conceded graciously, 'but in this case we're going to need special equipment appropriate to the situation, and we know you haven't had training in that. When we're ready to bring the lads out, it will have to be my team that does the job. No one else here has the authority to go down.'

Maggie could tell that the middle-aged GP was frustrated by his failure to get his own way. It had probably been years since anyone had gone against his authority, especially since he'd become the senior partner at the Penhally surgery.

Idly, she noted that while he was leaner than either Adam or Mike—almost thin enough to squirm through the narrow entrance to the adit. That was probably because he had lost muscle tone since his age had stopped him being an active member of a rescue team. Even so, it wouldn't be easy for him to get into the adit until the entrance had been cleared, to say nothing of the problem he would have once he got to the bottom of the stope and had to clamber over the rockfall and squeeze his long legs into the narrow tunnel where Tel was trapped.

'Well, I hope you don't think you're going to be stopping me going down again,' Maggie interrupted before Nick could draw breath to argue, suddenly aware with every fibre of her body that Adam had come to stand behind her. She hadn't seen him move but somehow she just knew that he was there, silently supporting her in her fight to do what she knew had to be done. 'Until you get that entrance cleared, I'm the only one small enough to get through who's got the training to take care of Tel.'

Not that she wanted to go back into the darkness again, feeling as if all that rock was pressing down on her and squeezing the breath out of her so that she had to fight for the oxygen her body needed to survive.

'I'm afraid I *will* have to stop you,' the team leader said firmly. 'The last thing we need is amateurs bumbling about when everything is so unstable. Because time is of the essence, we've only done a makeshift job of shoring up the entrance to the adit. We've made a start on clearing the access and it won't be long before the entrance is safely open again. Then we'll be able to take our equipment down and—'

'So while you're running about up here doing everything by the book to satisfy health and safety requirements, you're quite happy to leave an eight-year-old boy down there in the dark, taking care of his injured friend who's bleeding heavily and in danger of developing crush syndrome?' Maggie demanded, so disgusted that he was even considering the idea, let alone trying to insist on it, that she didn't think twice about exaggerating Tel's condition if it made her point. 'I think not!'

'Well, I'm sorry, but I can't allow you to go back down,' he insisted. 'I know you're a qualified paramedic, but this is way beyond what you're trained for…it could even lose you your job if you go down there again against my advice.'

'In that case, I'll be looking for another job,' she said with scarcely a pang for the potential loss of a job that meant so much to her. She straightened her shoulders and tried to stand tall, knowing it was a futile gesture when everyone around her was at least a head taller but still hoping he would recognise how seriously she took her decision. 'There's no way I can twiddle my thumbs up here while the last of that unit of saline runs out and Jem is left alone and terrified because he doesn't know what to do for his friend if he develops an air embolus.'

She whirled back towards the entrance of the adit and there was Adam, exactly where she'd known he would be. 'Adam, I need to take some more saline down with me, and a backboard in case I manage to get Tel free before you can get down there. Perhaps there's some sort of crowbar I could borrow to shift the last couple of rocks. I'll also need a blanket to keep Jem warm…oh, and something for him to eat. He didn't make it home in time for his tea and must be starving.'

She paused to take stock, wondering what else

she needed that she'd be able to negotiate down that treacherous stope single-handed, and saw Adam exchange glances with Mike who then nodded and hurried out of the circle of flood-lights towards their ambulance to get the things she needed.

'Maggie, are you sure about this?' Adam asked softly when he turned back to her, careful to keep his voice below the sound of the generator so that it only carried as far as her ears. 'I know how much you hate going into enclosed spaces and I virtually blackmailed you into going down in the first place, so don't feel that you have to— What?' he demanded when she winced as he took her hands in his and squeezed her fingers.

'Dammit, Maggie! What's happened to you?' he exclaimed when he saw the ragged, blood-stained fingers of her protective gloves. 'What have you done to your hands?'

'It's not *my* blood, Adam,' Maggie reassured him as he stared down in horror at the state of her hands, and she knew that she was largely telling the truth.

Of course, there was no way she could have shifted all that granite without collecting a few scrapes and scratches, but she was touched that he should care that she might have been hurt. 'It's Tel's blood. Because he's trapped, I was having to use the Braille method of finding out where he was injured. I needed to find out where the blood was coming from…how serious the injury was.'

'How badly *is* he injured?' Adam asked as he helped her to strip off the shredded gloves, side-tracked into throwing her a furious glare when he saw just how many scrapes and bruises there were on her hands. She clenched her teeth in preparation for the pain as she doused them in antiseptic gel then struggled to pull on a fresh pair of gloves over the fierce stinging.

Silently, he handed her some more gloves to stuff into the appropriate pocket of her pack. 'Did the lad fall a long way?'

'He didn't just fall—he brought down some rocks with him,' she explained, strangely warmed by his anger on her behalf. It had been a while since anyone had really noticed when she was hurt and showed that they cared. Even Mike tended to shrug off work-related injuries as part and parcel of the job they did.

'He's got a goose egg from hitting his head and I'm hoping that's the reason why he's unconscious, because I couldn't find any obvious evidence of cranial fractures. I've put a collar on him and he's on his second unit of saline. So far, it doesn't look as if he's in danger of bleeding out. Several ribs were broken when the rocks landed on him. He was having difficulty breathing when I got to him, but once I shifted the weight off his chest, that improved, and there's no evidence of pneumothorax or flail chest. The other lads would have cleared the rocks earlier if they'd had light to see what they were doing. He's also broken the tib and fib in one leg but they don't feel massively displaced, so I think the blood loss is probably from several smaller gashes rather than anything major like an artery. There's moisture seeping down the walls of the tunnel, so it probably makes the blood loss look worse than it is.'

'Miss?' said a hesitant voice behind her, and she turned to see a woman aged before her time, her face gaunt and white under the harsh lighting as she stood there with her hands knotted together. 'They said you've been down the mine?'

'Yes, I have. I'll be going back down in a minute,' she added, suddenly not needing to ask the question to know who the woman was. 'You're Tel's mother, aren't you?'

She nodded. 'Amanda Lovelace. Mandy,' she supplied, then bit her lip before blurting, 'Please, tell me what's happened to my boy. You brought his three mates out with you. Does…does that mean he's—?'

'He's unconscious,' Maggie interrupted hastily, sparing her that dreadful final word. If she'd realised Tel's mother was here she would have made certain she hadn't been left so long thinking the worst. 'He fell and hit his head and he's cracked a couple of bones. That's why it's taking a bit of time to get him out—we need to get a stretcher down to him to carry him out safely, so we don't do him any more damage.'

'But he *is* alive? You're *sure* he's alive?' She grabbed for Maggie's hand with frantic fingers and it was difficult to control the wince as she, too, pressed on the cuts and bruises that were starting to throb mercilessly.

'He's breathing and his heart is beating,' Maggie reassured her with a smile, sticking to the basics. 'He's got a bump the size of a goose egg on his head and he'll probably have a monster headache when he wakes up, but—'

'Oh, thank you! Thank you so much!' Mandy exclaimed tearfully. 'He's always getting into scrapes with those other lads—takes after his big brothers, unfortunately, and his dad's never there when he's needed—but Tel's not a bad boy, not really.'

'Miss Pascoe?' interrupted the incident commander, clearly ready for the next round in the battle. 'I know you mean well, but I really must insist that you don't put yourself in any further danger. You must realise what the consequences could be for your employment.'

Maggie took a moment to promise Mandy that

she would be told as soon as there was any more news about her son, then she turned to face the man who was rapidly becoming her number-one adversary.

She knew he was only doing his job, but it wasn't making things any easier for her. It was taking everything she had to stop herself thinking about the danger she was returning to. She would be only too delighted to stay up here and keep the man happy, but she knew she didn't really have a choice but to go against his advice. There were two young lads down there, one of whom might still be bleeding from a wound she still hadn't found, and the other was probably counting every second and every eerie creak and groan while he was waiting for her to return.

'If losing my job is what it takes, so be it,' she said stubbornly, her conviction that she was doing the right thing strengthened immeasurably by the thumbs-up signal Mike gave her as he delivered the supplies she needed, and the fact that Adam was once more standing right behind her.

In fact, he was so close that she could feel the heat of his body radiating towards her and his breath teasing the vulnerable skin left exposed on the back of her neck by her eminently practical haircut. For one mad second she even contemplated leaning back against him, desperately needing to borrow just a little of his strength. Then she remembered, barely in time, that he was a married man and that she had no right to take anything from him, even on loan.

That realisation was enough to stiffen her spine and her resolve to do what was right.

'Feel free to report me for going against your advice if you must, but at the moment I'm not even on duty,' she explained, almost ashamed how smug she felt. 'My shift ended several hours ago, so now I'm just a member of the public who has a bit more training than most and just happens to be small enough to squeeze through very small spaces.'

The man sighed heavily, reluctantly conceding that he wasn't going to win the argument, especially with Adam and Mike backing her.

'Well, if you're that determined, you should be wearing one of these...' he handed her a bright yellow safety helmet and checked that it fitted her head properly '...and you might as well have one of these, too,' he said, and offered her a radio. 'It's the latest issue communication system—the new one that actually works for some distance underground—so hopefully you'll be able to keep us updated on how the lad's doing.'

'And you'll be able to let me know when your lot's on the way down to get us out,' she said, and tightened her grip on the neat piece of equipment as though it were a lifeline, realising that this one high-tech gadget might actually make what she was about to do just a little more bearable.

'By the way...' A sudden thought struck her as she was about to thread herself through the rough-edged gap in the rocks. 'Make sure you tell your team to take it slowly as they come along the adit. Part way along, one of the roof supports is hanging down. I hit it on my way in the first time, but I'm short enough not to have knocked myself out on it. Your team mightn't be so lucky. Then, just a bit further along, the ground drops away completely into a series of steep, ragged-edged steps. Apparently, it's called a stope, and if you're not expecting it…'

'Thanks for the warning,' he said with a wintry smile. 'We've actually got a contact from the Camborne School of Mines tracking down underground maps of the area. We were worried that we might have to find another way in if the entrance kept crumbling, but we've got the temporary shoring in place now, and it seems to be holding. In fact, we're hoping to have you all out before anyone at Camborne has the time come up with the goods.' He paused a moment and gave his head a single shake. 'I still don't approve of what you're doing, but…good luck.'

'Thank you…and thanks for this, too,' she said holding up the radio, then threw him a distracted smile, suddenly aware how quickly time was passing. It was totally dark now, and she had absolutely no idea how long ago it had been since she and Mike had driven into the field in their ambulance.

More to the point, how long had it been since she'd left Jem down there with Tel? However long it was, she knew it would feel a thousand times longer to a young boy, no matter how brave he was.

Adam was waiting patiently to help her climb back into the awful blackness and the fact that his was going to be the last face she saw was the only thing that gave her courage when her claustrophobia once more tightened its grip on her throat.

'Be careful, Maggie,' he murmured as he held her with rock-steady hands. 'Don't take any risks.'

'As if climbing down a mine isn't risky,' she retorted wryly. 'And you're the one who persuaded me to go in the first place.'

'Well, don't do anything to make me regret it,' he demanded, his voice suddenly fierce. 'It was different when you were under the train. I was there with you, close enough to pull you out in a hurry if it became necessary. If anything happens to you this time…' He shook his head.

'Then you'll have to get hold of one of these gadgets so you can keep tabs on me,' she said as she waved the new communication link at him, not wanting to think about how much distance she would be putting between them as soon as she entered the adit. Anything beyond arm's length might as well be a million miles because he wouldn't be able to reach her; he wasn't as bulky as Mike, but his shoulders were still far too broad and muscular to fit through the entrance yet. 'That way you'll be able to talk me through it, like you did before.'

'I'll do that…even if I have to mug someone to get it,' he promised with a grin, then his smile faded and his dark blue gaze became suddenly intent. 'Maggie, we need to talk,' he said, his voice heavy with unexpected meaning that made her heart give an extra beat.

'Not now,' he added hastily when she stared up at him in surprise and caught a glimpse of secret-filled shadows she hadn't noticed before. Were they something new or had she been so focused on her hurt over the way he'd treated her a year ago that she just hadn't seen them?

'There isn't time now,' he continued. 'I know you need to get back down to those boys, but promise me that as soon as this is all over… There are things I should have told you a year ago…about Caroline…'

'Caroline?' she frowned, not recognising the name immediately and resenting the intrusion of another woman into a moment that somehow felt as if it had been exclusively theirs despite the noise that surrounded them.

'My wife,' he said quietly, and the illusion of intimacy was shattered with the reminder that, apart from the imaginings of a teenager's rose-tinted summer fantasies, Adam had always belonged to someone else.

Adam watched Maggie's petite form disappear into the darkness and had to curl his hands into tight fists to stop himself grabbing hold of her to prevent her from going through that torture all over again.

That last glance she'd thrown at him over her shoulder had been enough to break his heart.

He knew just how terrified she was of going back into the mine—knew how hard it was for her to fight the irrational fear of being trapped in a confined space. The fact that she had been willing to jeopardise her job to return to the two boys she'd left down there was a prime example of the woman she was, and he couldn't be any more proud of her.

'Bloody woman,' muttered the incident commander, the two of them standing to one side while a serious start was made on clearing the blockage from the entrance. 'Give them a bit of training and they think they can take on the world.'

'So you think she'd be better off sitting at home, darning someone's socks and cooking his tea?' Adam asked blandly when he'd rather be ripping the man's throat out. How could he *not* respect what she was doing when it was so much a part of who she was?

'Well, you know as well as I do that there are proper ways of doing things,' the man agreed. 'Proper protocols that women seem want to ignore just for the sake of it…probably because their brains aren't built to see the logic of rules and regulations.'

'You think so?' Adam was seething now and it was a real effort to keep the lid on his temper. The man didn't sound as if his ideas had progressed beyond the nineteenth century, let alone the twentieth and into the twenty-first. 'So you're incapable of admitting that without Maggie's guts and determination you'd still have five kids down there? Are you so hidebound by your rules and regulations that you can't see that one of those kids could have been well on the way to bleeding out if she'd tamely waited while you worked out the proper way to gain access?'

He turned on his heel and positioned himself as close to the entrance of the adit as he could without getting in anyone's way in the hope that it would help with the reception of the radio signal when he spoke to the brave woman already forcing herself to confront her greatest fear for the second time that day.

He'd probably already said far too much, but the thought that such an arrogant idiot was casting aspersions on Maggie's courage was enough to make him see red. She deserved praise, not condemnation for bending a few rules, and if the man thought he would win any points by criticising her for doing what she thought was right, he certainly didn't know how much that pint-sized paramedic meant to him.

Maggie's spirits were low as she forced herself to squeeze through the entrance without disturbing the temporary supports, and she'd barely set foot inside the adit when she was seized by the almost unbearable need to get out as fast as possible.

It didn't seem to matter that she'd already spent time in there, finding and taking care of the trapped youngsters, and had climbed out again virtually unscathed with three of them.

This feeling was something different—a gut-deep conviction that something dreadful was going to happen if she went back down the rough slope ahead of her into the depths of the mine.

There was another torch in her hand to replace the one she'd left with Jem, but she knew just how puny the beam would seem once she left the light at the mine entrance behind and was surrounded by utter blackness.

'Hey, Maggie. How are you doing?' Adam's voice echoed strangely around her from the radio in her hand and she gave an involuntary sob of relief. She'd had her reminder that he belonged to somebody else, but she was so very grateful that he was there for her at the moment.

'You know that expression, "It's just a walk in the park"?' she asked as she ducked under the timber hanging down in her way. 'Well, this is more a walk in the dark, and it's not nearly as pretty down here.'

'So, just imagine the flowers,' he suggested, and she could actually hear a smile in his voice, could picture the way it always accentuated the lean planes of his face and made his dark eyes gleam.

There was a teasing, light-hearted edge to his voice as he continued. 'Don't tell me you do all that driving around and hadn't noticed that there are already daffodils out in most of the gardens around Penhally? Don't you just love living in Cornwall?'

'I'd love it better if they went round and filled all these holes up,' she muttered as she reached the top of the stope and her heart contracted with renewed fear as she contemplated the fact that this time she'd be making her way down hampered by the extra equipment she'd brought with her. She really didn't want to have to make the climb twice if she didn't have to—it would waste so much time and energy—but was it too risky to make it in one journey, laden as she was?

'Maggie?' Adam prompted, but his voice surrounding her was suddenly a distraction she couldn't cope with, not for the next few minutes. It was such a comfort knowing that he was close enough to be able to speak to her, but now she needed every ounce of concentration focused on getting back down to Jem and Tel.

'Adam, I'll need my hands free for the next part,' she told him, loath to cut the connection between them. While he was talking to her she could almost imagine that he was down there with her. 'I'll speak to you again when I reach the bottom of the stope and find out how the boys are,' she promised, then cut the signal and stowed the radio safely in her pack.

It was every bit as awkward as she'd expected and felt as if it took twice as long, but with Jem watching from the mouth of the other tunnel and carefully shining the torch at each step of the stope to help her on her way, anything other than continuing until she reached him wasn't an option.

CHAPTER FIVE

'How's Tel?' asked as soon as she reached the pile of rocks almost obscuring the tunnel mouth, her legs shaking so much that she had to pause a moment before she could attempt to clamber over the mound.

'He groaned a couple of times just after you took the others up,' Jem reported, sounding worried, 'but he hasn't woken up yet. Oh, and the saline's nearly all gone.'

'Hey, Jem, it's probably a good thing he hasn't woken up yet, otherwise he'd be in a fair amount of pain,' she reassured him, as she deposited the more cumbersome items of her load outside the tunnel, hoping that she wouldn't have to make any decisions about administering analgesia to a patient in severe pain before his head injury had been properly analysed. As it was, her initial conviction that he didn't have a significant brain injury was being tested the longer he stayed unconscious, but until they could get him out of there, there was absolutely nothing she could do about it.

Her first job when she joined the two of them in the cramped space again was to wrap an arm around Jem's shoulders and give him a hug. He'd looked so utterly relieved to see her again that she'd known just how terrified he must have been to be left down here alone with his unconscious friend. And it wouldn't have made any difference to his level of fear that staying had been at his own insistence. It had still been an amazingly courageous thing for an eight-year-old to volunteer to do.

'You've been brilliant,' she said simply. 'I wouldn't have wanted to be down here by myself, so I think you thoroughly deserve these.' And she handed him a couple of the energy bars someone had given her up at the mouth of the adit.

She smiled when she saw the way his eyes lit up, suddenly seeing him for the little boy he was. 'At least those should keep the wolf from the door until we can get to some proper food.'

'Great! Thanks! I should have been home for my tea hours ago,' he said, already tearing at the first wrapper, then sat out of the way with his back against the rough wall of the tunnel while she checked Tel over again and decided that she didn't yet need to replace the bag of saline with a fresh one.

Once reassured that his condition hadn't deteriorated in her absence, it was time to decide exactly how she was going to accomplish the next stage of her task—to get him clear from the rockfall and safely strapped onto the backboard.

Really, there was only one way…she was going to have to use the borrowed crowbar to lever the last of the big rocks aside—preferably without doing any further damage to his legs—then log roll him and slide the two halves of the backboard under him from either side before he could regain consciousness and start trying to move.

'Right, Jem, if you've finished fuelling up your engines, I'm going to need a bit of help here,' she announced. 'I'd like you to take the bag of saline as far away up the back end of the tunnel as you can without pulling the needle, and then keep an eye on the tubing so it doesn't get knocked about.'

'And I've got to make sure it's still high up enough so that the stuff runs down into Tel, right?'

'Exactly right,' she agreed, and saw him settled safely out of the way before she began to attack the remaining rocks, frustrated that she was going to have to leave the largest till last, when she'd have the least energy.

It was hard, dirty, painful work, especially as she laboured to shift the final boulder away from between Tel's legs, and she was close to tears by the time she hit her shoulder on the same rocky outcrop for the dozenth time without apparently shifting the lump of granite more than an inch or two.

'Would it be safe for you to move Tel's leg a

bit that way?' Jem suggested, gesturing with his hands after a moment's pause in which she tried to control the urge to scream her frustration. 'The rock looks a bit of a weird shape and that's stopping it moving the way you want it to go, but if you could shift his good leg over to the side a bit, you'd be able to tip the rock over like that, and…what do you think?'

Maggie rested her hands on her knees while she weighed up the pros and cons of Jem's suggestion. She would dearly have loved to ask Adam's opinion—the way she had when the two of them had been battling to staunch the bleeding of the young woman under the train—but this time the decisions were all hers. She would have to balance the possibility of doing further damage by moving Tel against the probability that she'd finally be able to release him and get him safely immobilised on the backboard.

'Let's try it,' she said and, suiting her actions to her words, angled Tel's uninjured leg out into the limited space in the tunnel, hopefully without moving his injured leg or his pelvis, to give herself the chance to attack the boulder from a different angle.

'Yay!' Jem cheered when her renewed effort with the crowbar finally sent the stubborn rock flipping over in the new direction as easily as though it were one of the fake polystyrene rocks seen on children's television programmes. Not content with rolling over once, the granite rolled a second time, only stopping when it cannoned into the opposite wall with a resounding crunch.

Maggie barely stopped herself from shrieking when the impact sent a shower of dust and rock clattering down onto the three of them, but luckily there weren't many pieces and the ones that hit them weren't particularly large.

'Now we've just got to move those little bits and you can fix his leg,' Jem pointed out cheerfully, and Maggie wished it was going to be so easy.

'How about you clear away these rocks while I get my stuff in here to deal with Tel?' she suggested. 'Now that I've finished shifting rocks with it, I can stick the crowbar in this gap here and, hey presto, it's a hook for the saline.' She suited her actions to her words, jamming the sharp point of the metal bar into the space between the rock wall and one of the ancient timber uprights, leaving the hooked end at exactly the right height to suspend the unit of saline. A quick check to make certain that the tubing wasn't kinked anywhere and that the needle was still positioned correctly in Tel's vein then it was time to deal with stabilising his broken leg.

'How are you going to fix it?' Jem demanded as he scurried backwards and forwards, collecting the scattering of loose rocks and stacking them against the side of the tunnel. 'When I broke my arm, I had to have a cast on, but you can't do that down here, can you?'

'First I'm going to find out where all this blood's been coming from. Depending how badly it's still bleeding, I might need to put a pressure bandage on it to stop it bleeding any more, then I'm going to splint his leg to keep everything straight and safe while we move him. They won't put him in a cast until they get him to hospital.' *If they don't have to take him to Theatre first*, she added silently, still not entirely convinced that the youngster didn't have other undiagnosed injuries. Her biggest fear was that the blow to his head had caused an intracranial bleed; that the reason why he hadn't started to regain consciousness was because the blood was collecting inside his skull and building up potentially fatal pressure.

'So, where are you going to get a splint from?' he asked. 'If we were outside, I could probably find you a piece of wood or a straight piece of branch from the gorse bushes at the entrance to the adit. Down here there's only rocks or those great big treetrunks holding up the roof.'

'That's why we're going to use his other leg as a splint,' she explained as she positioned Tel's legs side by side, checking again that he had good circulation in both ankles before she began to bandage them together at knee and ankle. Another quick touch reassured her that the binding hadn't compromised blood flow and then it was time to manoeuvre the two halves of the backboard into position.

'Hey, I saw them using one of these on TV!' he exclaimed when she brought it over the mound of rock into the tunnel. 'There was a programme with a helicopter crew flying all over the place, doing seaside rescues and then flying the injured people to hospital.'

'Well, I hope you were watching carefully, because I'm going to need your help to get Tel positioned properly,' Maggie told him, and wondered if he'd ever realise just how much easier this whole nightmare had been for her with such an amazing youngster down here with her. It would have been better still if it could have been Adam by her side, but...

'What do you want me to do?' Jem demanded eagerly. 'Do you need me to help you roll him over to slide it underneath?'

'Good guess,' she said with a smile. 'But, actually, we're taught a special way of rolling him that we can do with just one person, because you're going to need both hands to get the board in exactly the right place. OK?'

'OK,' he said, and the little frown of concentration drew his dark brows together the whole time she was explaining what she wanted, first log rolling Tel onto one side while concentrating on keeping the whole length of his spine perfectly aligned in case there were any hidden injuries, then reversing the procedure for the other side…the more difficult side as he'd landed far too close to the wall of the tunnel for her to position herself easily.

'Can you see how to clip the two halves of the backboard together?' she asked, wishing she could sprout another pair of arms to help him align them.

'Got it!' he crowed as they slotted perfectly into position and she lowered Tel carefully onto his back again. 'Now we have to strap him down so he can't move about, don't we?'

'That's right. Tight enough so he can't slip about but not so tight that we stop his circulation or his breathing,' Maggie agreed as she positioned the all-important wedges either side of Tel's head and secured them with a strap across his forehead. 'Then we can let the others know that we're ready for them as soon as— Oh, good grief!' she exclaimed scrambling for her pack and dragging the radio out. 'I forgot to turn this on again.'

'...you there, Maggie?' Adam's voice suddenly flooded the tiny space, in spite of the fact that it wasn't a perfect signal and there was a great deal of background noise. 'Are you all right, Maggie? Answer me, please,' he said in the tone of someone who'd been saying the same thing over and over again.

'Adam! Can you hear me?' she demanded, her fingers fumbling in her rush to speak. 'I'm *so* sorry, but I forgot to switch this thing back on when I got to the bottom.'

'You *forgot*?' he repeated, the disbelief so clear in his voice that she felt a guilty blush flood her cheeks.

'Jem was waiting for me and he's helped me to shift rocks, splint Tel's legs together and get him strapped to the backboard. Everything's ready down here, so as soon as the team can get in, we're ready to go.'

'That's good, because we're just about ready now,' he said. 'They'll be bringing down the stretcher with them. Is there anything else you need? Anything for Jem?'

'Just to get him out of here as soon as possible and let him tuck into his tea,' she suggested, and Jem nodded furiously.

'OK. See you soon,' Adam said. 'And, Maggie, this time don't switch the radio off completely, so we can contact you if we need to.'

She heard the little click that told her he'd cut the call and missed him immediately…wished there was a good reason to speak to him again, just to hear his voice. Instead, she retrieved another couple of energy bars and sat down beside Jem while they ate them in companionable silence.

'What sort of cast will Tel have?' Jem asked after a while. 'Mine was a green one. It was made of fibreglass, but one of the girls in the top class had a big hard white one.'

'That will depend on exactly what damage they find when they take the X-rays. He might just have broken the two bones in his lower leg, but if he's injured his knee as well, he might have to have a cast right up his leg.'

'Wow! Mine was only part way up my arm, like a long glove, and my thumb and fingers were sticking out at this end.'

'How did you break your arm?' she asked, and there was a brief pause before he answered.

'I fell,' he said briefly, hurrying on to add, 'And they said I'd broken a bone that sounded like a dog. A spaniel or a collie or something?'

She chuckled. 'You mean a Colles' fracture— in this bone right here?' She touched his radius, just above the wrist.

'A Colles' fracture,' he repeated with a nod, and she was certain that this time he wouldn't forget the term. 'And I had to keep the cast on for ages and ages. Weeks!'

'Well, your friend will have to keep his on even longer because the leg is weight-bearing, so we have to be certain that it's properly mended before he can use it again.'

'How long will that take?' he asked.

'Well, it varies a bit from person to person because some heal faster than others, but it's usually anywhere from about six weeks.'

'Six weeks!' He was wide-eyed at the thought and added with dawning delight, 'Does that mean he won't be able to go to school?'

'Oh, I doubt he'll miss much school.' She laughed. 'As soon as the doctors are sure that he's on the mend, he'll be back in class with you again.'

She'd been watching his face while she'd been speaking or she'd probably have missed the look of misery that replaced his former delight. As it was, she was forced to make a rapid reassessment of the relationship between the two lads sharing the cramped tunnel with her.

'Jem?' she began, then didn't know how to continue. She had absolutely no experience of dealing with children of any age, except those she was called to care for in the line of duty.

What if she made a complete mess of the next couple of minutes? 'How long have you and Tel been friends?' she asked in the end, settling for something non-confrontational.

There was a pause that only gave her suspicions time to grow and it was obvious that there was a fierce inner debate going on. Would he tell her what he was worried about or would he put her off with vague half-truths?

'Tel's *not* my friend.' Jem interrupted her thoughts in a low voice, glancing across at him as though afraid that the unconscious boy might hear what he was saying.

'He's not?' It was what she'd been expecting after his reactions during their recent conversation, but it certainly went against what she'd assumed, especially as Jem had been so insistent about staying down the mine while she'd taken the other three boys out.

'He's been bullying me…him and his friends,' Jem admitted, then looked as if he wished he hadn't said anything.

As an adult, Maggie knew that any form of

bullying was unacceptable, but she could still remember how strong the code of 'don't tell' could be in the playground. She'd been a teenager when she'd been a victim, rather than Jem's eight years, and the girls who had targeted her had used far subtler means of torture than physical violence, but the scars had probably been every bit as long-lasting.

She wrapped an arm around his shoulders to give him a swift hug and the space blanket she'd tucked around him made its familiar rustling sound. 'Well, I think they're idiots because you've been absolutely brilliant today. In fact, as soon as we're out of here, I'm going to find out how to put your name forward for a bravery award.'

'You can't do that,' he said miserably.

'Why not? I think you deserve it. I don't think many grown-ups would be brave enough to stay down here with one of their friends and they certainly wouldn't want to be here for someone who was bullying them.'

'No…you don't understand. I don't deserve an award because it was *my* idea to come down here in the first place. It's *my* fault that all this has happened…Tel getting unconscious and bleeding and Chris getting hurt and everybody having to do the rescue.'

This wasn't making any sense.

'If Tel and his gang were bullying you, why would you come down here with them? Did they force you to take them?'

Now that she thought about it, the other four boys were at least a year older than Jem. He was obviously a bright lad, so was *that* why the others had picked on him? Or was it something to do with the fact that he didn't have a father around to fight his corner for him?

'They didn't force me but…' He threw an agonised look in her direction. 'Promise you won't tell anyone…not even my mum. You can't tell, or it'll only get worse. That's what happens when you tell on bullies.'

There was that unwritten code of silence that allowed bullying to continue, just as it had in her own childhood, and Maggie found herself reverting to the similarly childish ruse of crossing her fingers behind her back as she nodded, knowing that she had no intention of keeping her word.

At the same time as she was persuading the youngster to tell her what had happened and why, she was making a mental note to have a word with the headmaster to let him know what was going on…that was another note to go with all the others she'd been making, such as the talk she was going to volunteer to give the pupils about women's changing roles in society.

'Tel and the others were going to take my bike…and it's nearly new because I only got it for Christmas. And I said I'd found this mine all shut up and empty and…and I told them it might have treasure in it and…and if I showed it to them, they couldn't take my bike.'

'And then Tel fell and got trapped and your torch broke and you couldn't get out again,' she finished for him.

He nodded, his misery obvious. 'But you won't tell, will you? You promised!'

Before she could compound her lie, the radio crackled to life.

'Maggie?' No matter how bad the reception was, she could tell it was Adam's voice. 'Can you hear me?'

'Loud and clear, Adam,' she replied, her heart doing the same crazy little jig it had when she'd been a teenager.

'The entrance is clear enough for the team to come down. They're bringing a stretcher down with them for Tel. Are you all OK?'

'Looking forward to getting out of here and having something hot to eat,' she said, sharing a grin with Jem. 'Remind the team to take it slowly. We don't want any more injuries.'

'Will do. See you soon.'

For several seconds after the end of the call she and Jem sat there, straining their ears for the sound of their approaching rescuers, but all they could hear was the distant throb of the heavy generator and the closer sullen drip of seeping water, punctuated by the intermittent creaks and groans of the old mine workings.

Maggie didn't say anything, but she would be absolutely delighted if she never heard any of those sounds again, and as for the sensation of being trapped in an enclosed space, she had a feeling that, after this experience, she wouldn't even be wanting to put her head inside her kitchen cupboard.

'I can hear them!' Jem exclaimed, his head sticking out from their tunnel entrance. 'And I can see light coming towards the top of the stope.'

Maggie could hear them, too, as she performed a quick check of Tel's vital signs. It looked as if the bleeding had stopped, externally at least. They wouldn't know if he was bleeding internally until they had some proper diagnostic equipment available once he reached St Piran's A and E. His pulse and respirations were still within normal ranges and his circulation was still patent beyond the broken bones in his leg, so there shouldn't be any danger that he'd lose his foot.

'They're coming!' Jem announced, almost hopping from foot to foot in one of the first displays of eight-year-old excitement she'd seen from him. 'They're coming down the stope much faster than we did, but that's probably because their legs are longer than ours.'

'As long as they can go up again just as fast, we'll all be happy,' Maggie said, but her thoughts weren't really on what she was saying, not once she spotted Adam among the team members approaching the heap of rocks at the entrance to their tunnel.

'Welcome to our humble abode,' she said wryly, as she moved aside as far as she could so that there was room for both of them to kneel beside Tel's unconscious figure.

It was strange to be working with him again. The only other time they'd been involved in caring for a patient together had been that awful afternoon under the train, and even though these circumstances were equally stressful, it was almost as if they could read each other's minds.

She watched as Adam performed his own survey of Tel's situation while she passed on the details of his condition since she'd reached him and what treatment she'd given.

'He hasn't regained consciousness,' she

pointed out with a significant glance in Jem's direction, and Adam took the hint, his concerned expression telling her that he was questioning the possibility of a bleed inside the youngster's skull, too.

The next few minutes were busy as Tel's backboard was loaded onto the high-sided stretcher and strapped firmly in position, the whole arrangement designed to provide virtually all-round protection for a patient while he was extricated from the mine.

The only thing that broke Maggie's concentration was the fact that every time Adam touched her—even something as accidental and simple as the nudge of his shoulder against hers or the brush of his hand—it was like an electric current racing through her body that was able to recharge her batteries in spite of the hours of tension that had drained them.

She was almost giddy with relief that their ordeal was nearly over and desperately needed to think about something else or she might make a complete fool of herself.

A quick glance around reminded her that Jem was still there, silently watching everything that was going on and patiently waiting for his turn to leave the cramped confines and start his journey up to his waiting mother.

'How's Kate been coping?' she asked Adam under cover of the instructions being fired backwards and forwards between the various members of the team.

Adam rolled his eyes. 'I think she'd have coped far better if Nick hadn't kept trying to throw his weight around. As soon as the entrance was cleared, he was trying to insist that he should be the one to come down to lead the rescue. He didn't seem to realise that he would be far more use if he stayed up on top and took care of Kate.'

'Until you pointed it out?' she finished for him, and knew she was right when she caught sight of a brief flash of white teeth as he grinned at her briefly.

'I reminded him that I'd lost my father in the same tragedy as Kate had lost her husband, and that having Jem in danger was probably bringing everything back for her. For heaven's sake, Nick's known the woman for years!' he muttered impatiently, barely remembering to keep his voice low enough so that Jem couldn't hear. 'He was probably at school with her. Who better to lend her some support?'

'Right, folks, we're ready to move,' announced a commanding voice at the mouth of the tunnel, and any chatter died away. 'Let's get that stretcher out of there.'

'Excuse me,' Maggie interrupted, and was hardly surprised at the long-suffering expression on the man's face as he turned impatiently towards her. 'I just wanted to ask that Jem be taken out first. He's been down here virtually alone for some of the time, and needs to get up to reassure his mother that he's well. I also think,' she added as the man beckoned the youngster out of the tunnel, 'that he's one of the most courageous lads I've ever met and I'll definitely be putting his name forward for a bravery award.' She gave his shoulder a pat as he slid past her in the cramped space and he smiled back at her, his eyes suspiciously bright.

'Hear, hear!' said Adam as Jem sidled past him, climbing over his feet, and patted the embarrassed lad on the shoulder before he climbed out over the pile of loose rocks at the entrance.

'*Gwir kolonneckter, mebyon,*' said one of the older members of the team, obviously praising the eight-year-old as he emerged at the bottom of the stope. Seth Tregonning had been a tin miner in his youth and was one of the few people Maggie knew who could speak the Cornish language that sounded just right in this most Cornish of places.

'What does that mean?' Jem asked, beaming from ear to ear as a member of the team adjusted a safety helmet to fit him for the journey to the surface.

'True courage, my boy,' Seth translated in the slightly sing-song accent of the region, and there was a general murmur of heartfelt agreement.

The team leader cleared his throat and

Maggie was amazed to see that he'd been as affected by his team's response to the youngster as any of them.

'Right, then, Seth, I want you to go up first with Jem because you'll be able to move faster than the two with the stretcher, and we don't want any hold-ups,' he said with a swift return to his former briskness, and Maggie dropped to her knees again to finish putting the last of her equipment away in her pack, determined that she wasn't going to be the cause of any delay in the evacuation.

'The rest of you,' he continued, 'follow the stretcher up and be ready to help to smooth the ride up that wretched stope. Remember that everything is rough and has the potential to crumble under your feet. Adam, I'll leave you in charge of making sure that Maggie gets out safely as soon as she's picked up her stuff. OK?'

Out of the corner of her eye Maggie saw Adam's long legs make short work of climbing over the mound at the entrance to the tunnel as he moved out of the way for the appointed team members to take opposite ends of the stretcher to start the journey back up to the surface.

In just a few more minutes…a quarter of an hour at the most…they would all be safely up in the fresh air again, with the wide night sky spread over their heads and a sharp February breeze bringing the scent of the sea in from the bay.

Then…what?

Adam had said that they needed to talk once this was all over. Did he mean tonight? Her heart gave an extra thump at the idea that he might suggest that she go back to his home. She had absolutely no idea where he was living. The local grapevine hadn't passed that piece of information around yet.

Unfortunately, everyone in the town knew where *she* lived—in the same cottage she'd shared with her mother—and most of them would know by breakfast-time if his car was parked outside her place overnight.

Except the whole idea that the two of them would be spending any more time together tonight was complete nonsense. Adam was a married man and would obviously be going back to his wife. Any conversation between the two of them would have to wait until he found time in his busy life.

'Ouch! Mind your knuckles, Pete,' called the stretcher carrier at the front. 'It's bad enough that we have to hunch over so we don't hit our heads, but this rough-hewn granite is evil stuff and your gloves won't stop you making a mess of your hands if you hit the walls on the way through.'

Maggie glanced up with a wry smile, her own aching hands testament to that fact, and was just in time to see the last man out of the tunnel—was he the one called Pete?—step awkwardly on a rock that Jem had missed, twisting his ankle and throwing him off balance.

'Careful, man!' warned his colleague, as he fought to keep the stretcher stable. 'Watch what you're doing with those big feet of yours.'

The poor man muttered a curse and lurched forward a couple of ungainly steps before he got his balance back, but in those few seconds his shoulder had cannoned into the abandoned crowbar that she'd set up to support the bag of saline.

As if it was happening in slow motion she saw the moment when the length of hexagonal steel pivoted against the ancient timber bracing the roof of the tunnel, wrenching it out of the position it had held for more than a hundred years and sending it crashing to the floor with a hollow thud, narrowly missing the edge of the stretcher on its way down.

Somebody swore ripely into the brief silence after the echoes had died away, but what happened next was something out of Maggie's worst nightmares as first one rock, barely the size of her fist, fell onto the dank floor, before tons of boulders followed it, cascading down in an avalanche that nearly deafened her in the enclosed space of the tunnel.

'No-o-o!' she shrieked, forced to scramble back into the depths of the tunnel as it began to fill with granite, shutting out the light of the torches at the bottom of the stope.

In pitch darkness and terrified that she was going to be trapped and injured just like Tel had been, she forced herself to retreat as fast as she could, her pack still miraculously clenched in her fist as she stumbled and ricocheted against the ever-narrowing walls.

Then, suddenly, the ground fell away underneath her and her head hit something totally unforgiving and the darkness became absolute.

CHAPTER SIX

MAGGIE groaned, wondering groggily why she'd woken in the dark and why she felt so awful.

Her head hurt…in fact, everything hurt.

And she was feeling so disorientated…as if her brain had been scrambled.

Had the ambulance been involved in an accident, or had she been injured by one of their patients? She'd escaped anything major so far, but attacks on ambulance staff by the very people they were trying to help were happening more and more, especially when the behaviour was fuelled by alcohol.

Or was she coming down with flu in spite of the jab she'd had in the autumn?

She reached out in the darkness to switch on

the bedside light…and encountered a rough granite wall.

'Maggie?' Adam's frantic voice crackled nearby and suddenly she knew exactly where she was and what had happened.

'I fell,' she croaked, terror stealing her voice as she remembered those last few seconds as the ground had seemed to disappear under her.

She didn't remember landing, but the heavy throbbing of her head and the sensation of wetness in her hair was enough to tell her that she'd hit her head at some stage in the fall. 'So much for the safety helmet,' she muttered in disgust, although she supposed that it had hardly been designed with falling down a mine in mind.

What other damage had she done? Serious damage? Head injury? Broken bones? Internal bleeding?

It was so hard to do an examination of her own body when she couldn't see a thing. It didn't matter whether her eyes were open or shut, the blackness was absolute so she would have to rely entirely on her sense of touch...and knowing which bits hurt more than the rest.

How long ago had it happened? How long had she been unconscious? Minutes? Hours?

It wouldn't really matter either way, she realised with a crushing sense of despair. It had taken several hours to find the boys and effect their rescue, and that had only been a matter of shoring up the entrance to the adit and clearing the fallen granite that had been blocking it. The rockfall blocking this tunnel was enormous, and the chances that the rescue team would be able to clear it quickly...well, there was no chance at all, she admitted grimly as the full horror of her situation flooded over her.

'Maggie, please...!' Adam's voice crackled again and only then did it dawn on her that wherever it was, the radio had also survived the fall. Did the torch still work, too? She'd put it in her pack with the radio to leave her hands free, ready to climb up the stope for the last time.

Suddenly she was desperate to find that

radio—her one link with the outside world. At least with the radio working she'd be able to speak to Adam and the dreadful all-encompassing blackness wouldn't feel so suffocating.

She nearly rolled over to begin her search. Only her years of training made her pause, fear of the possibility of permanent paralysis making her stay completely still for just a little longer.

She had no idea how far she'd fallen, would never have moved an inch further back into that claustrophobic tunnel unless she'd been forced to by the rockfall, so would never have known that the ground dropped away not far from where Tel had been trapped.

So it was a case of moving just one limb at a time while she did a terrified check to find out how badly she'd been injured, and with each limb cleared with little more than bruising to report, it was time to focus on her head and neck.

Her hair did feel wet, and there was a bruise forming…perhaps she and Tel would be able to compare matching his-and-hers goose eggs…

but whether the wetness was from blood or the water continuously seeping down the tunnel walls, she had no idea.

Her neck felt a little stiff, so she could be suffering the after-effects of whiplash from the blow to her head, but the vertebrae weren't making any nasty crunching sounds and didn't feel any different from when she'd rinsed her hair under the shower so many hours ago that morning.

Just the thought of a steaming hot shower was enough to make her whimper. It felt like for ever since she'd last been clean and warm. Every inch of her body felt cold and wet and covered in dust and grit.

'But, dirty or clean, at least it feels as if everything is in working order…more or less,' she whispered into the darkness. There was no echo to bounce back at her, but she refused to think the logical next step…that there wouldn't be an echo in a space too small to bounce sounds back at her. The darkness was bad, but at least it was allowing her to fool herself that she wasn't trapped in a space little bigger than a coffin.

'Maggie? Can you hear me?' Adam called again, and the note of utter misery in his voice sent her scrambling to follow it, using the sound to direct her search.

In the background she heard another voice speaking behind Adam's, warning him that the radio had probably been damaged beyond use or buried under the rockfall, preventing her from using it. She could almost hear the implication that she was probably similarly damaged or buried, and suddenly knew that she had to get to that lifeline before Adam gave up trying to speak to her and she was left completely alone.

'There!' she muttered eagerly as her fingers encountered the familiar fabric of her pack. 'Got it!'

In spite of the fact that it was pitch dark, she found herself closing her eyes as she concentrated on the pack, running her fingers over it as she pictured what was inside each of the compartments until she came to the fastening she'd last closed when she'd pushed the torch and radio in for safekeeping.

The radio was silent now, and her hands were

shaking uncontrollably as she tried to remember which of the many buttons was the one she needed to press before she could speak to Adam. It was imperative that she let everybody out there know that she was still alive...*before* they all gave up hope and went home.

'Maggie, *keresik*,' Adam called, his voice hoarse and unutterably weary, and her heart leapt at the sound of that old endearment. She could remember telling him that it had been her father's pet name for her mother, handed down through generations of their family from the days when they had all been Cornish speakers.

She'd teased him about his claim to be Cornish when his name was definitely Irish, as was the combination of deep sapphire blue eyes and dark hair. He'd told her the family tale that, instead of fleeing from certain starvation in the other direction, to America, the original Donnelly had come across the water at the time of the potato famine and married a beautiful Cornish girl who had taught him to speak Kernewek instead of Gaelic.

Maggie could also remember the first time

he'd called her *keresik*, the very first time he'd kissed her on her sixteenth birthday, and the way her heart had soared that he'd thought of her as his darling.

'Adam?' she croaked, her throat thick with dust and emotion. 'Adam, can you hear me?'

There were several seconds of utter silence that left her terrified that she'd left it too late...that everyone had given up all hope of finding her alive...and then the darkness around her was filled with a crackly cacophony of voices whooping and cheering in delight.

'Quiet! Please!' Adam ordered before demanding, 'Maggie? Are you all right?'

She was just so glad to be able to hear his voice that she was fighting tears. It was several seconds before she could speak.

'It's dark, it's dirty and I've just been deafened,' she complained when she could finally control her trembling chin.

'Just like a woman—always complaining,' teased one of the men, and she couldn't help joining in with the laughter at the other end.

'Joking aside, what injuries have you got, Maggie?' Adam asked, his tone telling her that he had switched into professional mode. 'Can you start at the top and work your way down?'

'I've got a bump on my head from when I fell,' she replied obediently. 'It's painful and it might be bleeding because my hair's wet, but there's no apparent underlying fracture. I was unconscious for a while but I have no idea how long.'

'About five minutes,' he supplied, but there was an edge to his voice that told her that it had felt a lot longer than that. Was Adam suffering from the same guilt as Jem, convinced that it was his fault that she was injured because he'd persuaded her to go down there in the first place? Had he forgotten that it had been her own decision to go back into the mine to finish the job she'd started?

'Apart from that,' she continued, knowing that this wasn't the right time to hold such a discussion, especially when there were so many other ears listening in, 'I've got various assorted bruises and scrapes but, as far as I can tell, no broken bones.'

'None? Are you sure?' he persisted.

'My X-ray eyes don't seem to be working very well in the dark,' she quipped, almost light-headed with relief. 'I promise to let you take some as soon as you can get me out of here, if you think it's necessary.'

'I'll bear that offer in mind,' he said dryly. 'Now, tell me, how much of the rock actually came into that tunnel?' Suddenly all levity was gone. She was right back in the middle of a situation that couldn't possibly have a happy outcome.

'I don't know,' she admitted, belatedly feeling for the torch she'd tucked in her pack. Somehow, not being able to see how dire things were had stopped her thinking about them, but if she was going to have a hope of getting out of this mine, she was going to have to turn some light on her situation.

Her throat was already tightening again as she pulled the cold, smooth cylinder out of her pack and felt for the switch, dreading to find out just how confined the space was around her. She wasn't certain whether the fact that Adam could speak to her on the radio would be enough to keep her claustrophobia under control if she was truly on her own.

She moaned and closed her eyes when she took her first look around her, her breathing instantly harsher and her pulse racing. It was infinitely worse than she'd imagined.

'Maggie?' Adam prompted, but she couldn't speak. There were no words to tell him.

'How far back are you in the tunnel?' he persisted, then switched to coaxing. 'Come on, Maggie, you said you're not even badly hurt. All you've got to do is tell us where you are so we can get you out.'

'You can't...' she whispered in despair, hardly caring that he might not be able to hear her. 'No one can get me out.'

He muttered a word that she'd last heard when the two of them had been trying to wriggle their way under the underground train. That time he'd just caught sight of the pulsing spray of bright arterial blood telling them that the young woman was mortally wounded. They'd both known that they'd had just moments to stop her bleeding before her heart stopped for lack of blood to pump around her body.

Well, she *wasn't* mortally wounded, but it would have been infinitely easier if she had been. The death she was facing could take many days before she finally succumbed to dehydration and starvation.

'Maggie Pascoe, where's your backbone?' he demanded sharply, surprising her with implied criticism and igniting a spark of anger.

'My backbone is in the same place as the rest of me, in a hole about the same diameter as I am tall with no visible exits except the one near the roof that I must have fallen down.' She drew in a sobbing breath but was determined that none of them would know how close she was to losing it. 'It looks as if that last fall sealed me in here as neatly as a pharaoh in a pyramid.'

Her words were received with utter silence, almost as if they'd all stopped breathing while they'd taken in the significance of what she'd been telling them...that, like a pyramid, this mine had just effectively become her tomb.

Then, because she knew she was going to cry for all the things she was never going to achieve in her life, she deliberately switched the radio off.

Dammit, Maggie! No! Don't do this! Don't give up! Adam railed inside his head.

It was so hard to stand there, unable to do anything to help with what was going on around him.

Maggie had effectively shut him out by switching off the radio and, after an initial bout of frantic activity to help clear enough space to position props above the entrance where the tunnel had been, he'd realised that he had to step aside and let the professionals do their job.

All around him the rescue effort had redoubled in pace, the space at the foot of the stope teeming with men whose single objective was to find a way of getting to the woman trapped inside the hillside.

She shouldn't have been down there at all, Adam reminded himself as his guilt mounted by the minute. If he hadn't persuaded her to go—virtually blackmailed her into it, using her sense of duty against her in the worst way—then she would have been safe now, up on the hill behind Penhally, trying to stay warm in the biting chill of a February night.

And at least one of those five boys would have died by the time the rescue team had reached them, he reminded himself, the latest report from St Piran Hospital fresh in his mind. Terrence Loveday's injuries had been minimised by Maggie's expert attention, his breathing eased by her physical exertions to remove the rocks against his chest and the danger of major blood loss and permanent injury to his leg averted by the fact she'd correctly stabilised the fractures and administered replacement fluids. She'd even accurately diagnosed the fact that his persisting loss of consciousness wasn't just a symptom of concussion but of a slow bleed inside his skull from a damaged blood vessel.

The message relayed down to him just a few minutes ago was that Tel was in Theatre, already undergoing cranial surgery for the removal of a blood clot and, hopefully, the repair of the injury that had cause it.

Previous experience of similar cases told Adam that the boy would probably spend several days in Intensive Care in an induced coma while they waited for the swelling to go down. Only when his condition stabilised would they withdraw the drugs and wait to see if he regained consciousness; only then would anyone be able to judge how much permanent damage had been done by his fall.

The other injured youngster—Adam thought Maggie had called him Chris—would require some delicate jigsaw work to realign the broken bones in the back of his hand, but while his rehab would probably be long and painful if he was to regain his full range of motion, it was a far from life-threatening injury.

As for the rest of them, apart from a few nightmares to come about being stuck underground in the dark, they seemed to have escaped scot-free.

And, of course, the thought of the boys suffering from nightmares took him right back to Maggie and the terrible price she was having to pay, and the only thing he could do was play the whole situation over and over inside his head, wishing he could go back and do just one thing differently.

The trouble was, how far back would that train of thought take him? To the conversation at the entrance of the adit, when he'd coerced her into going into the mine against all her instincts? To a year earlier and the events of that meeting in London and the first time he'd persuaded her to put herself in danger? Or should he go all the way back nearly a decade to his failure to return to Penhally when he had been drawn back so strongly?

He needed to talk to her about all those things, to explain the what, the why and the wherefore of each of them, but most of all he needed to take away the look of distrust in her eyes that had been there ever since she'd seen the photo on his bedside cabinet.

He sighed heavily at that memory and hoped that he would have a chance to tell Maggie about Caroline, cool, beautiful, elegant Caroline who, like every other woman he'd dated after he'd left Penhally, had been as unlike dark-haired elfin Maggie Pascoe as it was possible to be.

Except he hadn't realised that was what he'd been doing until he'd seen her again, sitting at the front of the lecture theatre when he'd walked in to substitute for his sick colleague.

He hadn't been able to believe his eyes when he'd realised who she was, and from the wide-eyed expression on her face, she'd been equally surprised…and delighted?

It had been hard to concentrate on that first lecture when all he'd been able to think about had been that there would be a coffee-break coming up in an hour and a half and he would be able to speak to her for the first time since she'd been sixteen.

Oh, he'd seen her in the interim, briefly when he'd returned to be at his mother's side while they'd waited to hear news of his father. It had been small consolation to either of them to learn that he had died a hero, helping to save the lives of the group of children who had been cut off by the tide that summer evening.

And so, after the memorial service in the church overlooking a deceptively tranquil sea, he'd helped his mother to pack up their lives and move across the country to be near the rest of her family while he'd returned to medical school—returned with an image of the commiseration he'd seen in Maggie's beautiful hazel eyes to console him and a determination that one day he would return to Penhally to find the woman she'd become.

'Adam?' said a hesitant voice, and all the hairs went up on the back of his neck.

'Maggie?' he said, horribly aware that almost everybody around him had frozen in position at the knowledge that the woman they were toiling to rescue had chosen to contact him again.

'I'm sorry,' she said in a voice that was far huskier than usual, probably as a result of the tears she'd been shedding in the silence of her isolation. She might think that she'd hidden the fact that she had been close to breaking point and had needed time to herself, but he'd known. The only thing he hadn't been certain of had been whether she would turn the radio on again or whether she had seen her withdrawal as permanent.

'You've got nothing to be sorry for,' he reassured her, the guilt that was warring with his relief that she was speaking to him again suddenly overwhelming him. 'It's *my* fault that you're in this position at all. If I hadn't twisted your arm—'

'Adam, *don't*,' she said wearily. 'I really don't want to spend the next…however long playing the blame game. *I* shouldn't have stuck that crowbar there. I should have made certain that I'd cleared the passage better so Pete couldn't trip, and so on, and so on. I just want…' There was a wobble in her voice that made a tight fist clench around his heart. He didn't trust that his own voice would be any steadier so he simply waited for her to continue in her own time.

'I'm sitting here in the dark,' she said when she finally broke the endless pause.

Horrified, he broke in, 'Dammit, Maggie, you didn't tell me the torch broke when you fell.' How much worse could her situation get?

'No, Adam. The torch is OK,' she reassured him quickly. 'I decided to switch it off.'

'Why?' He couldn't imagine anything worse than sitting in the dark, deep underground.

'Partly I did it to save the batteries in the torch, but mostly it's because that way I can fool my mind a bit…pretend that I'm not surrounded by millions of tons of rock and I… Oh, please, Adam, would you talk to me?' she asked in a small voice that nearly broke his heart.

'What do you want me to talk about?' he offered, willing to promise her anything. Heaven only knew how long it would be before she wouldn't be able to hear him any more. Every cell in his body rejected the idea of a world without Maggie in it…her courage, her empathy, her sweetness…but logic told him that there was very little chance that they would be able to move such an enormous quantity of rock in the short time available to them. It could take weeks in such an unstable environment, with every bit of excavation needing extensive use of props to stop it collapsing again. Was that why the mine had been abandoned in the first place?

'Anything,' she said, sounding so like the young girl he'd first got to know all those years ago that his own eyes burned with the threat of tears. Why had he wasted so much time before he'd come back to see her? If he'd returned before he'd met Caroline, the whole course of both their lives would have been so different.

'Tell me about your wife,' she suggested, almost as if she was picking up on his thoughts. 'Tell me about Caroline.'

His ears burned at the thought that all the rescuers would be listening in to such a personal conversation, but if that was what Maggie wanted, who was he to deny her? She deserved that and more.

'Where did you meet? Is she a doctor, too?' Maggie prompted, just as someone tapped Adam on the shoulder.

'Hang on a second,' he said, and turned to face the slightly bashful-looking man standing behind him.

'Doc, I just wanted to tell you that the rest of us have switched our radios off to give you some privacy. The only interruptions will be if someone's contacting us on this frequency from outside. OK?'

'Thank you,' Adam said, hoping he was far enough into the shadows for the heat of his blush to be indistinguishable. 'I'll let you know if there are any messages.'

'Oh, Lord, I'm sorry, Adam,' Maggie groaned. 'I honestly hadn't realised that the whole world was listening in. I'll just—'

'They're not listening any more,' he broke in quickly, afraid that she might withdraw again. 'It's just you and me, the way it was in the library on a Friday afternoon, remember?'

The sudden gurgle of laughter at the other end

was exactly how he remembered Maggie…*his* Maggie…the one who was full of laughter, not the serious, studious one that everybody else had seen.

'Until the headmaster came in and caught us,' she reminded him. 'If you hadn't lit the candles, he'd never have known we were up there.'

'We couldn't celebrate your birthday without lighting the candles on your cake,' he objected, remembering the sudden stab of fear when he'd seen the expression on the joyless man's face. He'd been so certain that he was going to be thrown out of school before he could take his final exams.

Then Maggie, his indomitable Maggie had piped up, 'Would you like a piece of my birthday cake, sir? It's chocolate with real chocolate icing.'

The voice coming out of the radio was repeating the words verbatim, and he burst out laughing. 'Only *you* would have dared to offer the old dragon a piece of cake when he was ready to breathe fire.'

'Ah, but, then, I was one of the few people who knew that Mr Pendragon had a seriously sweet tooth and couldn't resist chocolate,' she said smugly, her Saturday job, when she served the older man with his newspaper and a large bar of chocolate each week having given her the idea.

'Well, he certainly proved it that afternoon,' Adam grumbled, still sore that the treat he'd organised for Maggie had been so thoroughly hijacked by their headmaster. 'He ate nearly half of it and it was supposed to be for you.'

'It was the thought that counted more than the cake,' she said softly, her voice almost lost in the crackles. 'I knew Mum was upset about working late on my birthday, but I never dreamed that when I told you, you'd go out to the bakery in your lunch-break and bring a cake up to the library.'

He hadn't been able to believe it either. Buying a birthday cake for a sixteen-year-old certainly hadn't been the sort of thing most other seniors would have done, and if his classmates had known about it…or about the fact that, instead of taking advantage of an afternoon without lessons to start the weekend early, he'd been meeting Maggie up in the library for several hours of study…

About the only part of it that his hormone-ridden classmates would have applauded was the fact that on her sixteenth birthday, in the shadows behind the furthest library stacks, he'd finally found out what it was like to kiss Maggie Pascoe.

'That was my first kiss,' she said, proving that her thoughts had been following the same inevitable path.

She'd been so very young when he'd met her, captivated at first by her quicksilver mind and shy sense of fun. He'd thought it would be little more than a quick peck…a token to celebrate the fact that she had officially become a woman. What he hadn't expected had been that her lips would be so sweet, or that they'd cling softly to his as her arms had come up to twine about his neck, pressing her slender elfin body against his and setting off an unexpected firestorm inside him. It had taken all his self-control not to let things get out of hand and it had almost been a relief when the bell for the end of the school day had sounded stridently right above their heads.

He'd needed a long cold shower when he returned home that night, but he'd made a promise to himself that, however their relationship went, he wasn't going to rush Maggie. He was the older of the two of them and it was his responsibility not to rush her through the wonderment of growing up.

He was determined that, even if he had to suffer frostbite under the shower on a daily basis, he would keep his libido under control, limiting their sexual experimentation to the kisses and cuddles appropriate for someone who had never run with the fast crowd. Just because he was older and ready to take things to a more intimate level, it didn't mean that he had the right to rush her before *she* was ready to take that step.

Neither of them could have known what that year was to bring. At the time that the two of them were laughing, teasing, talking and kissing their way through a glorious Cornish summer they had no idea that the next time they saw each other would be at his father's funeral and the memorial service for all those who had lost their lives that day.

'I missed you when we moved away,' he said, only now realising just how deep that emotion had gone. It had been as if an essential part of him had been torn away inside and hadn't been put back until he'd walked into the staffroom at Penhally Bay Surgery and seen Maggie standing there.

CHAPTER SEVEN

I MISSED you when we moved away,' he said in the darkness, and Maggie's heart swelled inside her, sending warmth to every part of her.

She'd never known that before, thinking that when they'd moved away he'd instantly forgotten the skinny bookworm he'd given her first kiss to on her sixteenth birthday.

For months after he and his mother had moved away she'd waited and hoped that he would write to her, but when nothing had come all she had been left with had been the determination to work hard enough to be accepted at the same medical school he attended. In her teenage mind she'd pictured the day when she would be able to meet him on even ground at least, both of them medical students working towards the same goal. Perhaps then he'd finally realise that she was ready for more than kisses.

Except while she was making her plans, the one thing she hadn't counted on was that her mother would become ill. ◊

'Mum had cancer,' she said, and the stark words still had the power to wound.

'Ah, Maggie, *keresik*, I'm sorry. Once Mum moved back to be near her family we lost touch with what was going on in Penhally. How long…?'

'She was diagnosed just before I took my last school exams—breast cancer—so even though I got the grades I needed, I couldn't take up my place at medical school.' Even this much later she could remember the bitter turmoil inside her as she'd railed against fate.

Her mother had been the only relative she'd had in the world and because she'd loved her, there had been no way she could have left her to go through the misery of cancer treatment by herself. But that didn't mean that she hadn't mourned the destruction of all the plans she'd made for her future, not least the fact that she would once again be able to see Adam on a daily basis.

'What treatment did she have?' he prompted, and after years of reticence it was almost a relief to be able to talk about it with him. He'd actually met her mother and he was also someone who would understand what she was talking about without having to go into long and involved explanations.

'She had a radical mastectomy and they excised the lymph nodes, too.' She could still remember her shock when she'd seen her mother for the first time after the surgery. 'She looked as if she'd aged twenty years overnight,' she murmured, reliving her terror that her mother wouldn't survive the night, that she'd be left completely on her own to make her way in the world. 'The primary tumour was the size of a pigeon's egg and highly vascularised and every lymph node they took out seemed to be affected. She was an absolute mess by the time they'd finished.'

'Chemo?' he asked.

'By the time she called it quits she'd had everything they could throw at her,' Maggie said through a throat that ached with tears. 'The surgeon seemed so sure that they'd got it all, but somehow they'd missed a tiny tumour in the other breast, and it was one that didn't respond to the chemo she was on for the other one. By the time they found it and realised what it was...' She swallowed, recalling the day when her mother had sat her down in their tiny kitchen and told her what the oncologist had found, and what the prognosis was.

'It was very fast growing, very aggressive, and he couldn't be certain that there weren't others elsewhere in her body so he...' She dragged in a quick breath so that she could get the telling over with. 'He told her that they could hit it with everything they'd got, but the treatment would probably be worse than the disease and there was very little chance that it would be successful. So she'd decided that she would like to spend the time she had left with me rather than in a hospital ward with a load of strangers.'

It had been a strange time, full of memories recalled and memories made. A time when she'd delighted in driving her mother to all the places that had been special in her life and listening as she'd told the tales of people and incidents that had made her who she was. It had been a time when she had been very aware that her mother had been saying good bye to her life and all the things that had made it so rich, and it had obviously given her so much joy and such an air of peace that Maggie had decided that it was what she would want to do when her time came.

Except now she wasn't going to have that option, not since half a hillside had come cascading down and buried her before she was even dead.

Maggie shook her head and firmly pushed that thought into the darkest corner of her mind. She didn't know whether she had just a few hours left or several days…but, then, was that really any different to anyone else? To Walter Dinnis, for example? One minute he'd been living his life, happily retired and spending the afternoon with his wife, and then the next Betty had been frantically phoning for an ambulance to take him to hospital and Maggie had needed to use the defibrillator to shock his heart back into its proper rhythm.

So she wasn't going to sit down here getting more and more maudlin by the minute. She may not have the option of doing it in person, but she was going to do her best to revisit all the events and places that had meant the most to her in her mind. And along the way perhaps she could get the answers to all those questions that had been plaguing her for so long.

'So *that* explains why you didn't go to medical school,' Adam said with the air of someone who had discovered the secrets of the universe. 'When we met up in London, I couldn't believe that you'd qualified as a paramedic instead. You'd been so determined to do well in your exams that I was sure you'd be tapping me on the shoulder one day to show me that you'd made it.' •

Maggie burst out laughing. 'That's *exactly* what I'd intended doing,' she admitted. 'I had it all planned in my head.'

'And after your mum was gone?'

'I couldn't afford to do it,' she said simply. 'Medical training was just going to take to long and be too expensive without any finances behind me. I even thought about selling the cottage, but...'

'But it was all you had left of your family,' he finished for her, knowing how she felt without her having to say it. 'I think that was one of the things that stopped me coming back to visit Penhally—the fact that I would have to see our old home and know it wasn't ours any more, that someone else was living there in the place that held all my childhood memories.'

'And now you'll be going past it on almost a daily basis when you're out doing house calls. Is it still a problem for you?'

'Not going past it, no. It looks so completely

different because someone's painted the old stone walls white and stuck fake shutters either side of the windows.'

'Don't forget the fact that the windows are now plastic and the new front door is studded with fake iron nails,' Maggie said, and was rewarded with a chuckle.

'What on earth makes people think that sort of thing is an "improvement"? There was nothing wrong with it the way it was—an honest-to-goodness fisherman's cottage built of local stone, roofed in Delabole slate and with the original sash windows.'

'Well,' she said, deliberately broadening her accent, 'you know what us locals say about they incomers… all thur taste is in thur mouth,' she teased, and he laughed aloud.

'You're not wrong there. It seems to be happening wherever there's a pretty sleepy place with tiny cottages. Before you can turn around, there's a crop of multi-million pound mansions squeezed between them—second, third and even fourth homes, meaning the locals haven't a hope of buying a home within twenty miles of their families or their jobs.'

'Well, at least the outsiders are only there for the summer,' she consoled him. 'Most of those new houses are probably only used for a fortnight every year, and long before the autumn gales come, the population's back to just locals, and life returns to normal.'

'I take it you've seen it at its worst, as a paramedic?'

'And then some,' she groaned. 'There's been an annual influx of Society types when the big public schools break up for summer. For a couple of weeks there can be several thousand teenagers congregating on the sand at one venue or another, fighting with their enemies from a rival school, or with pupils from some of the local schools. And when you factor in underage binge-drinking and the fact that some bring drugs down with them, it can be an explosive mix.

'I presume the authorities have been taking steps to minimise the damage, in human terms, at least?'

'You mean, apart from drafting in almost every available policeman in the area to police the alcohol and drugs and imposing a curfew on the beaches?' Maggie laughed wryly. 'They risk life and limb trying to separate the warring tribes while we paramedics are playing piggy-in-the-middle taking care of the injuries and overdoes. Thank goodness for places like Padstow. There's more for people to do there; more entertainment and come very good cafés and restaurants, as well as a lot of more affordable accomodation.'

'So, when we get you out of here, would you like to go to Padstow for our celebratory meal?' he asked, and her heart gave a sudden leap.

'At least in February you'd be certain of finding something open in Padstow,' she said wryly, while she tried to find the words to clarify the situation. In the end, all she could do was ask point blank. 'Adam, did you just ask me out for a meal?'

'I must be more out of practice than I thought if you couldn't tell that was an invitation,' he complained. 'Perhaps I need to give it another go. So, have you got a favourite place, Maggie? Will you come out with me?'

It was such a tempting thought and would be the fulfilment of a dream she'd had since she'd been fifteen, but there was one enormous obstacle.

'Won't your wife mind you asking me out, or will she be joining us?' she asked pointedly, knowing she wouldn't be able to live with herself if she went against her personal convictions, and that included an absolute ban on having a relationship with a married man.

'Dammit, Maggie, I should have told you about Caroline—' he began, only to break off when there was the sound of a shout from somewhere behind him. 'Just a minute,' he said distractedly, his voice fading, and she could picture him turning away from the radio to speak to the man who'd hailed him.

She tried to listen in on their conversation but the reception wasn't clear enough. She couldn't even tell from the tone of their voices whether the news was good, bad or indifferent, and had to wait impatiently until he came back to her.

In the meantime, she was left wondering just what he would have said about his wife if he hadn't been interrupted. Were he and Caroline divorced? She felt a pang of guilt that she should feel the remotest bit happy that he should have gone through that sort of misery. But it *would* mean that he was no longer married, a small voice inside her head pointed out.

Or perhaps they were merely separated, each resigned to the other's peccadilloes, uncaring that they were breaking their sacred vows. Unfortunately, that wouldn't change the situation as far as she was concerned. She believed that married was married, and only death—or divorce for those who believed in it—would change that.

'Maggie?' Adam's voice brought her out of the realms of speculation and the new energy that flowed out of the radio was almost visible. 'Someone's unearthed a map.'

'A map?' She couldn't see quite what the excitement was about. Most people might have completely forgotten that this mine had ever existed, but it was bound to have been marked on old maps.

'Young George used a few of his contacts,' Adam continued, and Maggie smiled the way she always did when she heard the old man's title, knowing it had been bestowed on him when his father and grandfather had both been alive.

'So how does that help anything?' she asked, frustrated that their conversation had been interrupted for something so unimportant. 'We already know where the mine is.'

'Ah, but this isn't the sort of map you're thinking about, with roads and railways marked on it,' he explained. 'This is a map that shows all the tunnels and whether they were adits, drifts, winzes and so on, and what level they all are in relation to each other.'

Suddenly she felt a spark of excitement, too. Did this mean that there was a chance they could find another way in to her living tomb?

'So, what have they found out?' she demanded eagerly.

'Not a lot, yet,' he admitted. 'But I didn't want to keep you in the...um...I just wanted to let you know that even though it might not seem like it at the moment, things *are* happening.'

'You nearly said you didn't want to keep me in the dark,' she pointed out with a quiver in her voice, not certain whether she wanted to laugh or cry.

For just a moment she'd thought it was all going to be easy, that with this old map they'd found there was another way to get her safely out of there, another adit coming into the mine from the other side of the hill perhaps.

Adam's narrowly averted slip of the tongue would have been funny under any other circumstances. It was only now, when she was so close to the edge, that it had nearly been enough to break her control, and that was the last thing she wanted.

If...when...the inevitable happened, he was bound to feel guilty for having persuaded her to go into the mine in the first place. He would probably ignore the fact that she'd willingly gone back down after she'd brought the three boys out, and take all the blame on his own conscience. He certainly didn't need to hear her fall apart, too. The least she could do was show the world some composure in the face of adversity.

'So...' She had to pause to clear her throat and pray for some inspiration. The one thing she *did* need was to have Adam close to her, because hearing his voice was enough to make her feel a little less alone. All she had to do was think of a topic.

'Did you ever hear what happened to the girl under the train? Joanna?' she asked, her brain instantly connecting the present situation with the first time she'd been in a cramped and dangerous situation with him. Then it had been his deep voice washing over her, instructing, calming, encouraging, that had helped her to cope with the whole thing on a minute-by-minute basis.

'I went to visit her a few days later on Orthopaedics, after she'd had some reconstruction work done,' he said, and as soon as she heard the smile in his voice she knew that there had been a successful outcome even before he told her. 'They'd managed to pin and plate her arm and done some microsurgery on blood, tendons and nerves, but she knew she was going to be looking at several more procedures to maximise function before plastics would make it look prettier. *But* she still had her arm and they were very optimistic about the outcome.'

'Did she tell you what had happened?' she demanded. 'All I heard was the rumour on the platform—that she'd screamed and jumped, and he was a good-Samaritan bystander that she dragged off with her—but while we were under the train, she didn't sound in the least bit suicidal. She was begging us to save her life.'

'Apparently, the man was an ex-boyfriend who wasn't taking the "ex" part very well,' Adam said. 'She said she'd realised just in time that he was a complete control freak who was systematically taking over her life, cutting her off from all her friends and family. She'd told him it was all over, but he didn't want to let her go.'

'So he decided that if he couldn't have her then no one could, and he pushed her under the train?' Maggie couldn't believe it. 'And to think I felt sorry for him!'

'She was just amazingly lucky that she landed between the rails without touching the live one. He had wrapped his arms around her before he jumped so even though she was struggling, he actually kept her fairly safe.'

'Except for her arm,' she said with a shudder, remembering the extent of that injury. When she'd first seen it, she'd been convinced that the wheels had gone completely over the arm and severed it. It had only been when she'd been trying to staunch the arterial bleeding that she'd realised that it had only been a particularly bad open fracture.

'As near as they could make out, the back of his head was hit by something under the train.

The blow destroyed the dens on C2—you probably know that's called the hangman's fracture—and he was dead almost instantaneously. Her arm was caught by part of the machinery underneath, too, but it wasn't a total traumatic amputation so the surgeons were able to salvage the hand.'

'So it was all worthwhile, being shoved under the train when I just wanted to run screaming into the distance,' she said wryly. 'The London underground system was hard enough to cope with, especially at that time of day with so many commuters packed onto the platform, but climbing down onto the track and seeing the tiny space I was going to have to squeeze into…' She shuddered at the memory.

'But you did it, because there was no one else small enough with the right knowledge to be able to save her life in the few minutes there was left to make a difference,' he said quietly. 'And I don't know whether I ever told you but I was so proud of you for being able to make yourself do it.'

'The way *I* remember it, you didn't really give

me much option,' she grumbled, to cover up the delight flooding through her at his words. She'd been delighted that Joanna had still been alive by the time the air ambulance staff had arrived with replacement fluids and the pain relief that she'd needed. At least she could console herself that her efforts had kept the young woman going until her care had been placed in other hands.

Once their help was no longer needed, Adam had suggested that she might like to avail herself of his bathroom to clean herself up a bit and that had been the moment when she'd realised that she had been covered in so much of Joanna's blood that she'd looked like a victim herself.

Of course, that wasn't the only reason why she accepted his offer so readily. If she was being honest, a large part of her eagerness was due to the incredible attraction that had been drawing the two of them together all day.

From the first moment that she saw him walk into the lecture room Maggie knew that Adam was still the only man for her. It may have been years since he'd left Penhally but she'd never forgotten him, measuring every man she met against his impossible standard.

It was hard to concentrate on the lectures while she watched him pace backwards and forwards at the front of the room, his body more heavily muscled than when he'd left as a teenager so that his shoulders looked broader than ever, his stride long and smooth. And those stunning eyes! She'd never seen another pair such a deep sapphire colour, or any eyes that held the sparkle that his did when he smiled at her.

Looking back on it, there had probably been several disgruntled women on the course, upset that he'd made it obvious that he'd wanted to spend his break times only with her. At the time all she'd been aware of had been the fact that she had actually been there, sitting next to Adam Donnelly, and that he'd seemed every bit as pleased to see her.

So when he suggested that she come home with him, there was no thought in her head that she would turn the offer down. In fact, it was quite possible that her brain ceased working altogether, handing over control of the evening to her heart.

The maisonette was bigger than she'd expected, bearing in mind the cost of housing in London, but other than that, inside it seemed like a typical bachelor's abode, with that morning's dishes washed but left on the drainer and a pile of opened mail on the table. The bathroom was no better, with the towel he'd used slung over the shower door rather than hung on the rail and the toothpaste and brush left on the back of the basin.

'At least I put my dirty laundry away,' he muttered defensively as he did a lightning tour, picking things up and putting them away before he found a clean towel for her and left the bathroom.

Her clothes had disappeared by the time she finally turned the shower off and she shivered at the knowledge that he might have seen her through the screen while she had been under the shower, hoping that he'd liked what he'd seen. Her only regret was that she hadn't known he was looking so that she could have invited him to join her.

Just the thought of being so wanton made her blush and she groaned at the fact that she'd had so little experience, afraid that it might turn Adam off. The trouble was, she'd never been so attracted to another man that she'd wanted to share her body with him. It had always been Adam for her, first, last and always.

The pale grey sweats he'd left just inside the door were far too long for her, but that was the perennial problem for her when she bought clothes, too. Anyway, she thought as she picked her shoes up while her heart tried to pound its way out of her chest, she was hoping that she wouldn't be wearing them for very long. If the expression in his eyes was anything to go by, Adam was every bit as excited as she was to be there together at last.

Perhaps it had something to do with the life-or-death events on the underground, making the two of them feel that they had to celebrate the fact that they were alive and well in the most basic way possible, but she'd barely stepped out into the hallway when he appeared from the tiny kitchen.

'Can I get you anything while your clothes are in the washing machine? Tea? Coffee? Something stronger? Or would you rather have something to eat?' he offered, but she barely heard him, her eyes feasting on the naked chest displayed to perfection above jeans worn white in prominent places.

She was struck dumb by his sheer masculine beauty and all she could think was that she only wanted to feast on him.

'Maggie…!' he groaned, and she knew that he was every bit as desperate for her as she was for him.

Suddenly it was so easy and so blissfully simple as she walked into his arms and offered her mouth for his kiss.

Within seconds he'd swept her off her feet and into his arms but she had no idea where he was taking her, only that his kisses were even better than she'd remembered, sweeter, deeper, more exciting, stirring her to her depths and re-verberating with all the emotions she'd been storing up for just this moment.

She'd thought that she would be shy the first time a man explored her body with love-making in mind, knowing that her slenderness was far from most men's ideal, but this was *Adam* touching her, stroking all the way up her shower-warmed belly as he pushed the borrowed sweat top up until her naked breasts were revealed.

'At last,' he breathed as he lavished attention on them, stroking and kissing and suckling them the way she'd longed for him to do that far-off summer. 'I've been wanting to do this for so long. You've no idea how hard it was for me to resist you back then.'

'So why did you bother resisting?' she demanded, while her brain was still in command of her mouth. 'You must have known that it was what I wanted, too, and once I was sixteen…'

'That's far too young to start a sexual relationship,' he growled, momentarily distracted from feasting on her. 'I was already eighteen and my hormones were driving me crazy, but even then I knew that it was too soon. You were too young to know…much too young for me to tie you down.'

She knew that he was right. Logically, sixteen *was* far too young, but in her heart she knew that if you met the right person at that age, there was no point in looking any further. All those years ago she'd been absolutely certain that he was the right person as soon as she'd got to know him, and now, finally, they were going to be together the way they always should have been.

He groaned as she arched her body up against him and tilted her hips, pure instinct telling her that he would find the pressure and friction against his aroused body impossible to resist.

She was right.

It took him only seconds to strip those jeans away and her eyes widened at her first look at his aroused masculine perfection before he returned to her and drew her into his arms.

She offered her mouth for his kiss but he hadn't finished speaking and touched a gentle fingertip to her lips while he met her gaze. She was disappointed for a moment, but the tension she felt thrumming through his body told her that this was just a brief delay. Well, she'd waited for years to experience his possession for the first time, so a few more minutes wouldn't make any difference, not when every inch of his body was silently shouting its intentions.

'Maggie, you do understand, don't you? I had to give you the chance to see something of the world...' he said with a concerned frown drawing his brows together, but she was far more interested in the fact that his dark eyes were slumberous with arousal and that the pulse at his throat was racing while he tried to continue their conversation. 'You deserved to have the opportunity to achieve the goals you'd set for yourself before you were tied down to a permanent relationship. I didn't want you to resent me for taking that away from you.'

'Stupid man,' she whispered lovingly as she

rubbed her naked breasts against the dark silky hair across his chest. 'We could have done it all together, helping each other through it. Just think of all the years we've wasted because you didn't think I was old enough to know my own mind.'

'You're sure you know it now?' he challenged as he plucked at the sleeves of her borrowed top, helping her to slide her arms out one at a time. 'No doubts about what you're doing?'

'None!' she declared triumphantly, and flung the sweat top aside.

A sudden clatter told her that she'd knocked something over on the bedside cabinet and, afraid that it might have been broken, she craned her head to look as he reached out to pluck the garment now draped over the bedside light.

'Did I damage anything?' she asked, mortified that she'd been so clumsy. Had she completely ruined the mood with her awkwardness?

'Nothing's broken and nothing's touching the light to be set on fire,' he confirmed, setting a silver picture frame on the surface again.

From the corner of her eye she caught sight of

the two sets of images frozen in time. One was obviously a photo of Adam and his mother taken on his graduation day, both of them smiling widely, but the other… She gasped in shock when she'd realised what she was looking at.

'W-who is that?' she demanded through suddenly chattering teeth, all thoughts of seduction gone as she focused on the bride and groom cutting the cake in the photo, each of them smiling widely for the camera.

The groom was undeniably Adam, impossibly handsome in his dark suit and white shirt with a blood-red rosebud in his lapel, and the tall elegant blonde beauty with the wealth of tumbling blonde hair…?

'That's Caroline,' he said heavily. 'My wife.'

Maggie didn't remember much of the next few minutes.

She knew that Adam had pleaded with her to stay, just long enough for him to explain…but he should have known that no explanations would excuse what he'd nearly enticed her into doing.

Yes, she'd been only too willing to go to bed

with him, but that had been when she'd believed that he was as free as she was to give her love—she hadn't known that he was married and that she was about to commit adultery.

The next thing she remembered was slamming the door of his house behind her with her handbag in one hand and her shoes in the other, dressed in nothing more than borrowed sweats.

Maggie never knew whether he'd tried to come after her that night once he'd put some clothes on, but presumed that he couldn't be bothered when there was no further contact from him, even though he knew she was going to be returning to Penhally.

That had been the last time she'd seen him until that afternoon, when she'd had to turn to face her nemesis.

The Penhally grapevine being what it was, she'd heard that he was returning to work as a locum and had been dreading their first meeting, expecting to hate him or, if not that, to at least despise him for the fiasco a year ago.

Instead, she'd found that her body and her heart didn't care what he had done, they still loved him as much as ever and desired him more than any other man.

She stifled a sob at the realisation that it was all too late.

Even if she'd been able to overcome her scruples, she was never going to know what it felt like to be possessed by him in that ultimate pleasure. The chances that she would be able to escape from the mine were so slim as to be neg-ligible and the chances that she would ever fulfil the dream that had haunted her for half her lifetime were non-existent.

CHAPTER EIGHT

TELL me about your wife…your blonde, beautiful, elegant wife…

The words hovered on her tongue yet again, but this time she wasn't so sure that she wanted to ask them.

She'd spent a whole year alternately congratulating herself for escaping from his house with her scruples intact—*their* house, she corrected herself with a grimace—and the other half wondering if she'd made the most enormous mistake.

What if she asked him now, when there was absolutely nothing she could do about it whatever he told her? What difference would it make to anything?

If he was still married she would die knowing

that Adam had never loved her the way she'd loved him, but if she discovered that his marriage had already been over that night a year ago, she would leave this life knowing that she had wasted the last year of it alone when the two of them could have been together.

'Adam…?' The voice in the background at Adam's end of the line called across to him again, and when Maggie realised that her chance for asking that question had disappeared again, this time she wasn't sure whether she was disappointed or relieved.

Then the voice drew closer…not close enough for her to follow their conversation but enough for her to realise that it was some sort of update about Tel.

'I don't know if you heard any of that,' Adam said when he returned to her. 'But that was a message from Neurosurgery at St Piran's. Tel's out of Theatre and is being transferred to ICU as we speak.'

'So he did have to go to Theatre,' she said with sudden feeling of dread. 'How much did I miss? Have they been able to rectify it?' At first she'd been quite certain that Tel didn't have a major cranial injury, but when he'd shown little sign of regaining consciousness her concern had steadily grown. 'How is he?'

'You were right to be worried,' he said. 'I passed your suspicions on so that the neurosurgeon was waiting for him when he arrived at St Piran's. Apparently, Tel did have a small bleed at the site of the cranial trauma that they only picked up when they did a scan. They went in to remove the clot to relieve the pressure on his brain and to make sure that the injury wasn't still bleeding, and then orthopods did a swift job on his leg.'

'And? What's his prognosis?' For Jem's sake she didn't want Tel to suffer any lasting damage. She could imagine the youngster taking it hard, even though it hadn't been his fault.

'With the usual proviso that the next few hours are crucial, they're pleased with the way it all went. Everything's looking good, and the chances are that he won't have suffered any per-manent damage,' he reassured her, and she breathed a sigh of relief as he added. 'They also sent their compliments for a job well done to whoever patched him up and stabilised him.'

'Well, this is definitely my day for collecting pats on the back,' she joked, touched that the staff at St Piran's would send such a message. All too often in their job, the paramedic's contribution was forgotten almost as soon as the patient was handed over in A and E. It was gratifying that her work had warranted a special mention, especially considering the conditions she'd been working under.

She was also delighted to hear that Tel was expected to make a full recovery. Of course, there was always the usual caveat about the initial hours after surgery, in case there were any unforeseen setbacks, but he was an otherwise fit and healthy boy, which had to augur well for his recuperation.

She'd been lost in her thoughts for a while and only realised that Adam hadn't spoken for some time when she heard the indistinct sounds of a heated discussion going on in the background at his end of the radio. She even thought she heard him shouting at someone, although he'd always been the most easygoing of men, far more likely to walk away from an argument than get into a pointless fight.

'Adam? Are you there?' she called. 'What's going on out there?'

'I'm here, Maggie,' he replied immediately, but sounded slightly distracted, as though a large part of his attention was elsewhere. That impression was confirmed when he added, 'Hang on, *keresik*. I'll get back to you in a minute.' And to her horror he broke the connection between them with an audible click.

The next few minutes seemed to stretch into infinity while she waited for him to come back, and she'd even resorted to watching the illuminated seconds ticking away on her watch to prove to herself that time hadn't stood still.

'Gone midnight,' she whispered to the surrounding rock walls, and tried to imagine just how many millions of midnights had passed since this hillside had been formed. As far as she could remember from her geography lessons, granite was an igneous rock formed in conditions of intense heat during volcanic activity.

She smiled at the thought. Cornwall, land of volcanoes? Not! ∤

Except…now that she thought about it, hadn't someone once told her that St Michael's Mount was an ancient volcanic plug isolated out in Mounts Bay, and what about Launceston Castle? That high motte could easily have the remains of another volcano at its heart. How many more could there be that she'd never really thought about before, and how could she find out about them?

Penhally Library might have the information, just a few doors along from Nick Tremayne's house. Or, failing that, there was always the internet…

Her excitement died a sudden death when she remembered that visiting the library and surfing the net probably weren't on her agenda any more, so she'd probably never know whether there really were any volcanoes in Cornwall.

'No!' A sudden surge of anger seized her. She might be stuck down here until…for the foreseeable future, but there was no reason why she couldn't ask someone else to find out for her. Even if they didn't have immediate access to a computer, someone among the large rescue squad assembled such a short distance away must know someone who did… Or perhaps Young George knew the answer without having to consult reference books? His schooling might have been short and basic and he'd gone into mining immediately after that, but his knowledge of the industry was encyclopædic, as was his familiarity with Cornwall and all things Cornish.

'So, that's what I'll do,' she said aloud, her new determination filling the little man-made cave around her. 'As soon as Adam comes back to me, I'll ask him to speak to Young George about the volcanoes in Cornwall.'

As if her words had brought it about, there was a sudden click and crackle and her heart leapt with the knowledge that Adam had switched the radio on again.

'Maggie?' His voice sounded husky with weariness and, instead of leaping in with her planned question, she found herself wondering just how many hours he'd been working that day. Had he been on call last night, too, or did the surgery use an out-of-hours service to prevent the GPs burning out?

'*Keresik*, are you there?' he called urgently, and she realised she'd been so wrapped up in her concern for him that she hadn't replied.

'Where else would I be?' she said wryly. 'I tried to do "Beam me up, Scotty," but the Star Trek transporter-thing that came free with my breakfast cereal the other morning doesn't seem to be working.'

His chuckle emerged close to her ear, almost as though they were sharing a pillow, and wrapped itself warmly around her.

'That's one of the things that I loved about you all those years ago,' he said reminiscently. 'It didn't matter what happened, you always managed to bounce back and find a joke to lighten the atmosphere.'

'Well, I'm struggling a bit this time,' she admitted. 'Now, what was all that about a few minutes ago? Tell me you've got some good news.'

'I don't know what sort of news it is,' he confessed, serious again in an instant. 'All sorts of experts have been looking at this old map—by the way, the mine was apparently called Wheal Owl at one time. Unfortunately, there seem to be as many opinions as there are experts.'

'Not unlike a medical conference, then,' she cut in wryly. 'So is there a general consensus?'

'Unfortunately, no,' he admitted. 'Because we don't know exactly where you ended up when you fell, so there are at least two possibilities.'

'And?' she prompted when he paused, knowing there was more to come and dreading the premonition that the bad news was about to get worse.

'And both of them are under a layer of particularly dense granite that would take for ever to break through, and as it's sandwiched between softer strata, there's a danger that—'

'A danger that the softer layer would collapse

before you could get me out and I'd have the whole lot land on top of me,' she finished for him, able to visualise that happening all too easily after seeing what had gone on at the mouth of the tunnel.

'Keresik?' he said when the silence had begun to feel as if it would stretch for ever. 'Are you still speaking to me?'

'Oh, Adam...' She sighed despondently, suddenly aware just how hopeless this all was. 'Are you all wasting your time out there, trying to find a way to do the impossible? Would it have been better if—?'

'No!' he snapped fiercely, not even giving her a chance to finish the sentence. 'We *are* going to get you out of there. It's taking longer than any of us wants, but we're going to find a way.'

Once again there was an interruption from somebody talking to him, just when she needed his undivided attention to bolster her flagging spirits. Without the torch on she felt, strangely, as if she had her claustrophobia under control— up to a point—but it wouldn't take much for the whole situation to overwhelm her and send her into a full-blown panic attack.

She swallowed down her fear, wondering just how much further she could keep it under control. She was tired and thirsty and it wouldn't be much longer before hunger kicked in with a vengeance, too, and all she had to look forward to was the last remaining unit of saline and one more energy bar. If ever there was a time when she wished she carried some extra weight, this was it—her body could have lived off its own stores for a while.

'So, what are the possibilities?' she forced herself to ask. 'Where do they think I am?'

'Well, it can't be a winze but it could have been an exploratory tunnel…along a rider that didn't go any further.'

'A winze? A rider?' she repeated, not having a clue what he was talking about. Jem would probably have known.

'I'm sorry. I'll say it in English,' he said and began again. 'It can't be a winze—a shaft between levels for ventilation—because the map shows that this mine never went below one level. But it could be a passage that was cut to follow a mineral vein that they thought was a rider—a thin seam of ore lying above a larger seam. You might be in a vertical cut that they were dropping down in the hope that they'd hit a big seam somewhere below.'

'How would they know?' She briefly flicked the torch on, squinting against the sudden brightness as she played it over the closest rock walls. She certainly couldn't see anything that looked like a seam of ore—it was all the same rough blotchy indeterminate grey with rusty-looking streaks where water had constantly seeped through over the years.

She switched the light off again, shutting out the image of the walls surrounding her so closely, preferring to try not to think about them.

'Tin occurs naturally as tin dioxide in rock called cassiterite, and the miners would have recognised the tinstone, as they called it, and brought samples up for assay to determine the percentage yield. That way they would know whether it was economically profitable to extract, and therefore worth following the seam any further.'

It made sense. Unless the whole mine had suddenly ceased operation for some unexplained reason, this could easily be the end of a failed exploration...of a failed mine. It certainly didn't go any further than where she was sitting. 'And the other option?'

'That it could be a sump or sink.'

'And they are?' she prompted when the explanation wasn't immediately forthcoming, wondering at his sudden reticence when he'd been only too keen to explain mining terms a moment ago. His strange reluctance was still clear when he began speaking again.

'Some mines were plagued with underground springs or surface water that would drain down through the workings. So, to make sure that the area where the miners were digging wouldn't flood—which would stop them working a full shift when it rained—there would sometimes be a drainage pit or pool excavated to draw the water away.'

'So I could be sitting in something that was part of the underground drainage system?' It was fascinating, but it would all be so much more interesting if she were watching it on television rather than viewing it in person. It would be nice to have some colourful diagrams to look at, illustrating the terms he'd been telling her.

Either way, she did remember learning that it was an important part of Cornish history that stretched back through the years when Cornwall had produced half of the world's tin plate and boasted the world's largest copper mine, all the way back to Phoenician traders who had come to barter and the prehistoric settlers who had first discovered and extracted the minerals.

'So this hole could actually be full of water sometimes?'

'Exactly,' he said shortly, and the unexpectedly clipped tone sent all the hairs up on the back of her neck.

'Adam, what *aren't* you telling me?' she demanded uneasily.

He was silent for so long that if she couldn't hear the slight crackle on her handset she would have thought he'd cut the connection again.

'Adam, *please*,' she said quietly. 'I need to be able to trust you to tell me the truth…now of all times.'

'I'm sorry, *keresik*, you're right,' he admitted soberly. 'I just didn't want to put any more stress on you.'

'You may as well get it over with,' she said. 'Once I know the worst…'

'Maggie, the weather report is forecasting a band of rain moving across Cornwall later on today. Heavy rain, and it'll probably arrive by midday.'

'Oh…damn!' she choked. 'And I was going to do some washing today.'

'Ah, Maggie, don't…'

'I know. It was a poor excuse for a joke,' she said, but it was better than breaking down while he was listening.

She drew in several deep breaths and blew them out slowly while she fought down panic.

She'd thought things were as bad as they could be, living right in the middle of her worst nightmare, but they had just got much worse. Until now she'd had hope to cling to. There had been a chance that one of the mining engineers could come up with some way to get her out of there if she was just able to survive long enough on saline and an energy bar, but if she drowned in the meantime...

'Adam, can we talk about something else? I really don't want to—'

'Anything you like,' he offered quickly, apparently every bit as eager to change the subject as she was. Well, she couldn't blame him. Talking about her imminent death wasn't exactly a cheerful topic of conversation.

'You never told me how you and Caroline met,' she said, and was almost certain that she heard him groan.

She nearly took the question back, wondering if this was the sort of conversation that would be of interest to a woman but would bore a man to tears. Then the stubbornness that had got her through her mother's illness, without once breaking down, kicked in. ▸

Adam had started to make love to her a year ago, before she'd caught sight of the photo taken at his wedding to Caroline and had run barefoot into the street. The least he owed her was a conversation about the woman she'd nearly had a part in dishonouring.

'Was she a doctor, too? Did you meet during your training? Or was she completely unconnected with medicine?' she prompted, then leant back against the dank support of the rough granite and made herself as comfortable as she could, totally prepared to wait him out until he spoke.

Adam stifled a sigh at her determination. Maggie was nothing if not persistent, always had been, but he hadn't been looking forward to this conversation.

If, God forbid, Maggie didn't survive this disaster, nothing would have been gained by raking over that whole miserable episode in his life, but if she came out of it in one piece, his marriage to Caroline was something that she needed to know about if there was any possibility that he and Maggie were to have a life together.

Ha! It had all seemed so easy when he'd been planning it, once he'd got his head around the fact that Maggie had stormed out like that, unwilling to stay long enough to listen to him.

He hadn't been able to leave London straight away but, then, he'd decided it was probably wiser to give her time to cool down. First there had been the situation with Caroline to resolve, and that had taken all his determination and concentration for several months and had left him utterly drained.

Then he'd seen the advertisements for a locum post at Penhally Bay Surgery and everything had suddenly come together in his head. He'd still had his contract to finish in London, but he'd decided that if he applied for a job in Penhally and got it, even though it was only supposed to be temporary…

If everything went wrong, it would only be a matter of weeks before he would be leaving

Penhally for good, but hopefully it would give him enough time to mend his fences with the only woman he'd ever loved.

Then what? He'd propose, they'd get married and live happily ever after?

As if anything was ever that easy! Look at where they were now, and he'd only met her again that afternoon.

Well, he'd wanted to tell her about Caroline a year ago, when she'd first seen the photograph, so even though he knew that some parts of the story didn't show him in a very good light, there really wasn't any reason not to tell her now.

'I met Caroline just before I qualified,' he told her. 'She was a trainee midwife in Obs and Gyn when I was doing my rotation there as part of my GP training.'

'And?' she encouraged, and he briefly thought that this felt far worse than when he'd had an impacted wisdom tooth removed.

'And she got pregnant, and we got married,' he added bluntly, not proud of the fact that he'd probably just shocked her, but they were the basic facts.

'But…but you *were* in love with her?'

He could almost hear her pleading with him to agree, but he couldn't lie to Maggie just to keep her belief in happily-ever-after intact. If she wanted him to tell the miserable tale, she was going to get the whole of it, warts and all.

'I was in lust with her, certainly,' he admitted, still shamefaced about his shallowness. 'You saw her in that photo. She was a beautiful woman.'

'Was?'

He stifled a smile as he leant his head against the rough stone wall, his body curved around the radio to give their conversation a semblance of privacy in the noise and chaos surrounding him. Any other woman would have been ranting at him for being so superficial, but not his Maggie. She'd homed in on the one really important word in the whole sentence.

'We weren't really in a relationship at that point. It was just one of those things…a party and too much to drink…' And every day such a deep unrelenting feeling of loneliness, an emptiness inside that had never been filled in spite of the fact that he had been surrounded by people enjoying themselves in one of most sophisticated cities in the world. 'And a few weeks later she was standing there, telling me that she was pregnant.'

For a short while he'd hoped that marriage to Caroline and the fact that they'd had a child on the way would finally banish the loneliness, but before he'd been able to find out…

'We bought the maisonette at auction—a decent-enough sized place for that part of London—but the only reason we were able to afford it was because it was in such a dreadful state. The elderly gentleman hadn't been able to take care of it for years so it needed absolutely everything done to it…ceilings, walls, plumbing, electrics, new bathroom, new kitchen…the lot. And the last thing on the list, after all the really dirty jobs were finished, was to put a new carpet on the stairs.'

He could still picture that frayed old carpet, an

indeterminate grey with all the dirt and dust that had been trodden into it during the weeks that the work had been going on, and with ugly thread-bare patches at the front edge of every step.

'I was going to take the carpet up that weekend and we were going to have a ceremony to celebrate replacing it with a brand-new one, only somehow she tripped on one of the thread-bare patches.' He dragged in a quick half-breath, needing to get to the end of the tale. 'I watched her fall down the stairs and saw her hit her head on the newel post.'

He heard Maggie's gasp of shock. 'Oh, Adam! How badly was she hurt? And the baby?'

'She lost the baby that night.' His tiny daughter had barely been as long as his hand, her lungs far too premature for her to survive. 'Caroline was in a coma. The scan showed a subarachnoid haemorrhage from an aneurysm. They discovered that she'd had an arteriovenous malformation in her brain that had probably been there from birth. Totally asymptomatic, so no one had known it was there. The bleed was large and catastrophic…there was massive irreversible damage to her brain.'

He would for ever blame himself that he hadn't sorted the carpet out sooner, but working on Obs and Gyn in a busy London hospital had meant long days and feeling permanently exhausted.

'If she'd been born with that malformation of the blood vessels in her head, the bleed could have come at any time,' Maggie pointed out, entirely logically. 'It could have been as a result of a car crash—even a relatively minor shunt if it whiplashed her brain inside her skull—or if she'd been mugged, it could have had exactly the same outcome. It could even have happened while she was in labour if her blood pressure had risen. Adam, you can't blame yourself. It was a disaster waiting to happen.'

'I know that in my head,' he agreed. 'My medical knowledge tells me that the chances that she'd survive into old age were extremely slim, given the fragility of those veins and arteries and the stresses that everyday living was putting on them. But that doesn't stop me from feeling guilty, from feeling that if only I'd taken the carpet up just one minute earlier...'

'I know all about those "if only" thoughts, the ones that go round and round inside your head interminably,' she said, and when he heard the sadness in her voice he knew that she was thinking about her mother. 'If only Mum hadn't got cancer,' she continued, and the connection between them felt almost as if he'd read her mind. 'If only she'd gone to the doctor sooner. If only the doctor had seen the second tumour before it had a chance to metastasise, and so on and so on. But if you go down that road...'

'But you can't just forget it, as if it never happened,' he objected.

'No, but you can gradually put it in perspective by remembering all the good things that happened before that.'

'Has it worked for you?' he challenged, marvelling that they'd slipped almost seamlessly into the same sort of relationship that they'd had so many years ago. Once she'd got over her painful shyness around him she'd become the one person in the whole of Penhally with whom he'd felt able to discuss absolutely anything without worrying how she would react.

'For the most part,' she said thoughtfully and, as ever, honestly. 'Some days are worse than others, of course. When something fantastic happens—a good save on a shout, for instance—and she's not there when I arrive home, bursting to tell someone about it.'

Now he felt guiltier still, because he and Caroline hadn't even had *that* sort of relationship, even though they'd been married. They'd been more like two small planets each confined to their own separate orbits.

'So, when we met up last year, when you were substituting for the other lecturer?' Maggie began again, clearly determined to have everything straight in her head.

'Caroline was still on life support then,' he admitted, 'but only because her mother couldn't bear to let her go. The woman I married was dead—she'd probably died within minutes of her head hitting that post—and that was several months before I saw you sitting at the front of that lecture hall.'

He was almost holding his breath as he waited for her verdict but knew better than to try to rush her. Maggie would take her time to assimilate everything he'd told her and then she'd make up her mind whether she was going to forgive him…forgive the two of them. He couldn't bear it if all he was to have of her was the memory of the only time he'd held her in his arms, kissing her without having to hold back, knowing that she'd wanted him as much as he'd always wanted her.

'I was a fool,' she announced flatly, clearly angry with herself, but all he felt like doing was letting out a cheer. 'If I hadn't leapt to conclusions…'

'Maggie, legally I was still married until the machines were switched off and she was pronounced dead,' he pointed out, acting as devil's advocate but needing her to address all the facts, not least the truth that they would, technically, have been committing adultery.

'But you would have told me that if I'd given you a chance, wouldn't you?' she said with a depth of trust in her voice that humbled him. 'If I hadn't leapt out of bed full of self-righteous indignation and raced out of your place like a lunatic, you would have told me all of this then.'

CHAPTER NINE

'MAGGIE?' Adam called, and she was surprised to discover that she'd actually been dozing.

Was she actually becoming accustomed to being in such a claustrophobic place with the rumble of excavation work going on non-stop somewhere not too far away? Or had it been it a combination of the utter darkness surrounding her combined with sheer exhaustion that had allowed her to shut out the world for a little while?

She gave a sharp laugh of disbelief that she could actually have slept away some of the precious time left to her. It was now…gone two o'clock in the morning, she noted from her watch, and the rain was due to arrive before midday. That meant that she had, at most, just—

'Maggie, are you awake?' he called again a little louder, and something in his voice told her that he didn't just want to chat to her to pass the time away.

'I'm awake,' she confirmed as her stomach rumbled loudly, reminding her just how many hours it had been since she'd last eaten. Still, there was one good thing about not having enough to eat or drink…she didn't need to go looking for a bathroom—at least, not just yet. 'What's been going on up there? Have the experts come up with a workable plan between them?'

'No. Not yet,' he admitted. 'But they were hoping you could tell them about the rocks that make up the walls where you are, to see if they can pinpoint it more accurately.'

'OK,' she said dubiously. 'But I don't really know what I'll be looking for. The last time I did any geography was at school, and the amount of geology I remember would fit on a postage stamp. Granite just looks like granite to me, but I'll give it a go.'

It took several minutes before her eyes were

accustomed to the light and she had to deliberately switch her mind off to the fact that the
walls she was inspecting were within arm's
reach in any direction, but she still couldn't see
anything remarkable anywhere around her.

'I'm sorry,' she said. 'Some of it's stained
brown where the water's been running down
it and there are those glittery metallic flecks
all through it, but I can't see anything that
looks like a band of anything different. In fact,
some of the loose rocks on the floor are more
interesting—there are some lovely examples
of iron pyrites.'

'And you said you didn't know any geology.'
He laughed.

'Well, everyone's heard of fool's gold,
haven't they?' she said.

She ran her fingers over a particularly pretty
chunk while Adam was reporting her lack of
success to someone in the background while she
mourned the fact that she wouldn't be able to
give Jem a piece of it as a souvenir of his heroism.

'Maggie, exactly how much loose rock is

there? Enough to pile up and see if you can look back along the tunnel?'

'I can only see the entrance to the tunnel from here because it's up at roof height…above my head. I think you're forgetting that I'm one of the shorter people of the world,' she complained.

She heard him repeat her words and was startled when instead of laughter she heard someone seeming to get very excited at what she'd said. There was another heated discussion going on as she started collecting the larger chunks of rock to pile them directly below the aperture she could see above her head. It was galling to think that Adam would probably be able to reach it without even going up on tiptoe, but if she was going to be able to have a look along it, she was going to have to do some hard work first.

'Maggie?' called Adam.

'Hang on!' she panted. 'I'm still building the Great Wall of China.'

'Well, let me know when you've got it high

enough for you to be able to pull yourself up into it. Are there enough rocks for that?'

'There should be…some of them were pretty huge, and damn hard to land on,' she complained. 'It's a good job my head was harder.' She had no idea why everyone was suddenly so keen that she stick her head into this tunnel, but if there was the slightest chance that it would help them to get her out of here, she'd use every little scrap of granite to build as high as they wanted her to.

'OK,' she said, and briefly crossed her fingers that the whole shaky edifice wasn't going to collapse as soon as she tried to put any weight on it. 'It's time to go mountain climbing.'

'Be careful, *keresik*,' he said softly. 'Don't break anything.'

It wasn't until she was perched precariously on the top of the little cairn she'd constructed that she could see that there were actually two tunnel entrances opening into her little prison. One of them had been completely out of sight behind an overhang.

She climbed down to report her findings and an even more animated discussion erupted at Adam's end.

'Is there any way you can talk to us while you're looking into each of the tunnels, to describe what you're seeing.'

'Yes, if I grow another arm,' she joked, trying to work out the logistics of holding onto a torch, the radio and having a hand free to steady herself against the wall so that she didn't overbalance. 'Hang on a minute. I've got an idea.'

She reached for her pack and found a roll of tape, pulling a length off to strap the torch to one wrist and the radio to the other. Now, if she could only point each in the right direction to be of any use…

'Right, one tunnel is bigger than the other and the floor of it is more gently sloping. I'm almost certain that it's the one that Tel was trapped in because there are an awful lot of loose rocks in it, as though they're the ones that rolled the furthest when the roof came down, and I can hear a lot of intermittent crashing and banging sounds coming from further along it, so that's probably where you lot are.'

It was such a relief to find out that she hadn't really fallen all that far and to know that *that* was the direction her rescuers would be coming from. Whether they would have a chance to move that much rock before the rain came was another matter, so she needed to give them all the information she could to see whether there was a quicker way to get to her.

She turned carefully, holding onto anything she could to steady herself one-handed as she shone the torch into the other aperture…and shuddered at what she saw.

'The other one is much narrower, not much wider than my shoulders, and probably too low to do anything more than crawl. That one slopes up and out of sight. It certainly wasn't the one I came down to get here.' And it definitely wasn't something she was comfortable looking at. She'd thought climbing under the train in the underground had been bad, but that tunnel was a sight to stop the breath in her throat completely...a living nightmare.

'Maggie, you've cracked it!' Adam exulted, exhaustion apparently a thing of the past. 'The boffins were looking at the map while you were describing what you could see, and they've pinpointed exactly where you are!'

'And?' Maggie held her breath, hardly daring to believe that there might be a happy ending to this whole disaster.

'And it looks as if you've just found your own way out,' he said, his words almost falling over each other in his hurry to get them out. 'What you've just described is an upcast...a ventilation shaft that was needed to bring fresh air into the area where the men were working and to dissipate some of the heat, so it led all the way from the mine out to the surface.'

'A ventilation shaft?' She looked from one tunnel entrance to the other. 'They both look a bit big for that.'

'That's because you're accustomed to modern ventilation,' he said with a smile in his voice.

'It's the same with modern mining. They could now drill a narrow shaft and put forced ventilation in, but the fact is, instead of the whole job being done with pick and shovel, much of the work is done by machinery run on compressed air, so that's being pumped underground at high pressure, and helps with regulating the air quality and temperature better.'

'But…' Her eyes widened as she looked back at that narrow shaft with the first awful presentiment of what was coming.

'In a mine as old as this,' he continued eagerly, 'the ventilation shaft would have needed to be bigger and would have been cut by hand by a man with a short-handled pick…or it could even have been a young lad all those years ago. You did say that it was just a bit wider than your own shoulders?'

'Yes, but…' She was having to fight so hard to breathe that she could barely form the words, her eyes mesmerised by the opening that seemed to be shrinking as she looked at it.

'Then *that's* the answer!' he exclaimed,

clearly delighted with the solution they'd come up with. *'That's* your way out of the mine.'

Her throat closed up completely, leaving her standing there, shaking her head wildly. She almost fell in her hurry to get as far away from it as possible, but even with her back pressed against the unyielding stone she was too close.

It had been bad enough making herself climb into the adit and knowing that five boys had already made their way through it recently. There had also been the spur to the professional side of her, knowing that at least one of them had been injured, possibly dying.

But this? It was totally impossible! She'd never be able to—

'Maggie?'

His call snapped her out of her blind panic, the tone of his voice telling her that it wasn't the first time he'd said her name.

'I couldn't,' she croaked, not caring that there was a shrill note of terror in her voice. Adam, of all people, knew how much trouble she had with enclosed spaces. He would understand that a tiny space like that would be a challenge too far.

'Maggie…it's the only way,' he said gently, persuasively. 'You're so slight that you'd easily be able to wriggle your way—'

'*No*, Adam, I *can't*!' She dragged in a shuddering breath. 'I'll just have to wait here until the rescue team can excavate the tunnel out again and…and pray that it doesn't rain too hard.'

'That's not an option any more, Maggie.' His voice was deadly serious. 'I couldn't tell you before, but they've failed every time they've tried to shore up the roof of the tunnel. That rock layer is so unstable that they'd be putting their own lives in danger if they were to continue. You can't expect them to do that if there's a viable option. Most of them are married men with families. It wouldn't be fair.'

'But…' Her eyes flew towards the larger tunnel, hidden behind that deceptive overhang, and she was close to tears.

She'd heard the sounds of excavation going on

and had been so certain that it was only a matter of time before they broke through the blockage and helped her out. To learn that the tunnel was now permanently blocked was a disaster, especially if her only alternative was to force herself to climb into *that*.

'Maggie, I know I blotted my copybook a year ago, but will you trust me one more time? I promise you, I'll be here for you every inch of the way and I'll be the one waiting at the surface when you come out at the other end.'

The thought of emerging into the freedom of a grassy hillside with nothing but the wide night sky over her head was so seductive, especially with the prospect of Adam waiting for her when she got there, but first she would have to go in there and...

'I can't do it,' she whispered as helpless tears began to stream down her gritty cheeks. 'Oh, Adam, I wish—'

'You *can* do it,' he argued fiercely. 'Trust me, you *can*. You're the strongest, most courageous woman I've ever known, and I love you.'

'You…' That was a completely different feeling of breathlessness. 'You *love* me?'

'Of course I love you,' he confirmed, with the simplicity of complete conviction. 'I've always loved you, right from when you were a shy little fifteen-year-old gazing up at me with those enormous hazel eyes and that incredibly generous heart. I wasn't in the least surprised when you told me you'd given up your chance at medical school to be with your mother, but I need you to do something for me now.'

'Something for you?' She was still reeling from his declaration. All these years she'd never known exactly what he'd felt for her; had believed that the love had all been one-sided.

'Yes, *keresik*.' There was a strange hoarseness to his voice that made her ache inside with the need to comfort him, but he was far too far away. 'I need you to trust me enough to at least give it a try, because I couldn't bear to lose you, not when we're so close to having everything we could ever want.'

'What if it's blocked?' she blurted, putting

one of her greatest fears into words. 'What if I were to get part way along it and there was no way out?'

'Then we'd start excavating from the other end until we got to you,' he said with utter sincerity. 'Some of the mining engineers are already on their way up to the surface to get to the other end of the ventilation pipe, to make certain it's not hidden in the middle of a gorse bush.'

This was so hard.

Well, in one way it wasn't hard at all. She desperately wanted to be out of the mine and wrapped in Adam's arms, but… It looked as if the only way she was going to get there was to thread herself into that horribly small ventilation shaft and inch her way up however far it was to the surface, praying all the way that there weren't any obstructions to stop her getting there.

'Can…can I think about it for a minute?' she asked hesitantly, all too aware that there was a large group out there who'd been up all night working to get first the boys and then her out of this old Cornish mine.

Then there was Adam, who'd been there for her right from the moment this whole mess had started.

'Of course you can, *keresik*, but, please, don't take too long,' he warned gently. 'We're all exhausted, you included, and there's that rain band getting closer with every hour.'

She hadn't really needed the reminder. She could hardly forget that she was facing the choice between battling against a phobia that could paralyse rational thought and even compromise sanity, and the alternative of drowning.

Her abject terror was so great that she knew she wasn't going to be able to stop herself sobbing out loud for much longer. There was only one way she could prevent everyone hearing her loss of control, so she deliberately broke the connection that had been her lifeline throughout the night and then switched off the torch.

She wasn't absolutely certain how long she wept, but one thing she did know by the time she'd blown her nose was that it hadn't done anything to help her make her decision.

That was purely down to one question—did she love Adam enough to want to spend the rest of her life with him, enough to trust him to do everything he could to take care of her and keep her safe?

'Of course I do,' she said aloud into the darkness, even as she quailed at the thought of what she still had to do to get to the security of his arms.

But the decision was made, and now she only needed to prepare herself for the task ahead.

Taking her pack with her on her back would be impossible…unless she could use a length of bandage to tether it to her somehow and drag it along the tunnel behind her. She'd already made certain that she wasn't going to lose the torch or the radio by taping them to her but…

'Oh, Adam,' she whispered into what had become a very eerie silence now that all work had stopped on trying to excavate the tunnel mouth. 'I do trust you, but how can anyone know whether this ventilation shaft will be clear all the way up?'

And if she were to get stuck part way? What then?

There would be no point in shuffling her way back down the shaft only to drown, but even though Adam had said that they would dig her out if necessary, the chances of that being successful—that she wouldn't be crushed by a rock-fall in the process—were pretty remote.

She buried her face in her hands, not liking where her thoughts were going but knowing that, if the worst came to the worst, it might be her only option.

She switched the torch back on and reached for the pack, knowing that there weren't any powerful opiates in it that would ease her way into the hereafter, but there was something else that might do the job just as effectively.

'Left side down, head down and legs up,' she murmured, voicing aloud the imperatives for preventing death by air embolism, knowing that positioning a patient's body that way would force the air accidentally introduced into the circulatory system to rise into the right atrium of the heart and stay trapped there, preventing it from entering into the pulmonary arteries.

She'd drummed the facts into herself during her training, knowing that as little as ten millilitres of air could be fatal for a frail patient. So far, she hadn't needed to use the information in practice and it was an awful thought that she was even contemplating reversing it as her fail-safe plan if everything went horribly wrong.

The prospect of lying there, trapped every bit as much as a body buried in a coffin, was too much to think about now, especially when she still had to bring herself to start that journey.

Even so, she grabbed what she would need and slid it into the top pocket of her uniform, knowing that once she was in the shaft it would be too late to second-guess herself.

Then, before she finally switched on the radio again and had the possibility of dozens of people listening in, she shuffled to the far side of her little prison and relieved herself with a wry grin.

'*That's* what I think of mines!' she muttered

as she pulled herself together again, disgusted with the state of her once-smart uniform. Then she reached for the radio to let Adam know that she was ready to give it a go.

'Maggie! Dammit!' he exploded, sounding half-demented by the time she spoke to him. 'Don't do that to me again! I've been going mad, not being able to talk to you…hear your voice… Lord! Let's get this over with! I need to hold you and I don't think I'm going to be letting go any time soon.'

'That sounds all right with me,' she said with a smile as she imagined how good that would feel—to be in Adam's arms, knowing that it was where she belonged. 'I shall hold you to it, but first I've got to pile up a few more rocks. I made the heap tall enough to look into the shaft, but not high enough to climb into it.'

It didn't take long to place a few more rocks on top because there weren't many more that she could manage, not without the crowbar that had triggered this whole situation.

There was another small piece of that same glittery rock she'd found earlier and she tucked it into her pack, actually looking forward to the time when she could give it to Jem as a souvenir.

'OK. I'm as ready as I'm ever going to be,' she announced, but suddenly she was shaking so badly that she couldn't even climb onto her little construction.

'Maggie?' Adam called, sounding far calmer than she ever could. 'Did you know that the children's corner in the surgery has got a book called *The Adventures of Molly the Mole*?'

'A children's book? In the surgery?' she repeated, nonplussed.

'That's right. But I think they're going to have to change the name soon. How do you think *The Adventures of Maggie the Mole* sounds?'

'Awful,' she said, but he'd made her chuckle and released her from the shakes.

This time when she went to climb up, it was as easy as if she were stepping up into the cab of the ambulance, ready to set off to the next casualty, knowing only the bare bones of the situation she was about to face.

Climbing into the shaft was every bit as bad as she'd thought it would be and she had to focus on the basic mechanics of what she was doing rather than where she was doing it.

The second her feet finally left the floor she froze for several long seconds, overwhelmed by what was ahead of her.

Her face was just inches from the rock. In fact, all of her that wasn't directly in contact with the granite was just inches away from it, and that situation wasn't going to change until she finally reached the surface…if she ever reached the surface.

She touched the contents of that top pocket through the fabric, almost as though touching a talisman. She didn't know whether she would be able to bring herself to use it, even if her situation became dire, but there was a grim sort of comfort just in knowing that it was there.

'How's it going, *keresik*?' Adam asked, his voice sounding strangely intimate in the confines of the shaft, reminding her all too clearly of his husky endearments when he'd taken her to his bed a year ago.

'Well, I've started,' she reported, not certain whether she should concentrate on what she was doing or whether allowing her mind to wander would make the time pass more quickly.

'And I'm up here waiting for you,' he said. 'We've found the top of the shaft.'

'And removed the gorse bushes around it?' she said, inching forward and upward, using her elbows, knees and feet to propel herself along, sometimes crawling, at other times forced to drop to her belly and conscious with every tug at her waist that her pack was following along behind her like a reluctant dog.

'No gorse,' he said. 'This time it was brambles with vicious thorns. I think the plant must have been here since the ventilation shaft was excavated because we nearly needed the jaws of life to cut through the stems.'

Maggie knew that he was keeping up the inconsequential chatter to help keep her mind off where she was and what she was doing, but the one thing that was keeping her going was the fact that he was there, waiting for her, and that he'd told her that he loved her.

She refused to contemplate the possibility that he'd only said that to give her the courage to climb this narrow shaft. He'd asked her directly whether she trusted him, and she'd known without a question that she did.

So, if he'd said that he loved her, then he did. The only thing she didn't know was what part he wanted them to play in each other's lives.

It was probably too soon to know. After all, they'd only met up again this afternoon—or rather yesterday afternoon, as it was now somewhere near five o'clock in the morning—for the first time since their event-filled meeting a year ago. Before that, it had been nearly ten years since they'd seen each other.

What if it was nothing more than the adrenaline overload that was making the two of them feel such an emotional connection…each of them apparently equally drawn to the person they'd known at a time when life had seemed so much safer and more settled and so full of endless possibilities?

Her internal debate seemed to have been going on interminably without any hope of getting any answers. How could she ask Adam what he thought when he was probably surrounded by members of the rescue squad standing by in case they had to start digging her out?

'Hey, Maggie the Mole, how are you doing?' Adam asked, and she couldn't help smiling at his nonsense. If nothing else, she was going to have to hug him just for keeping her spirits up.

'I feel a bit like a hamster or a gerbil, doomed to keep running for ever on a little exercise wheel, only in my case it's a rock-hard slope that's doing dreadful things to the knees and elbows of my uniform and— Ow!' she exclaimed when she didn't watch what she was doing and accidentally hit her head on a protruding knob of granite.

'What's wrong, Maggie? What happened?'

'Just hit my head,' she grumbled as she paused

in her seemingly endless trek. 'It wouldn't have been so bad if it hadn't been the same place as it got hit before.'

'On your goose egg?' he asked sympathetically. 'Ouch! I'll have to give it a kiss better when you get here.'

The kiss sounded a wonderful idea but she was beginning to wonder if she'd ever collect it.

'It's probably bigger than a goose egg now,' she told him as she rested her forehead on her hands for a moment, suddenly realising just how exhausted she was. 'You'll be able to see it on all the maps. "Maggie's Tor"—and it'll be twinned with Mount Everest.'

She heard him chuckle and it gave her the impetus to push onward the next few inches and the next until suddenly there was nowhere to go because she was confronted by a pile of rocks.

'Adam...?' she quavered, feeling sick. She'd come so far that she'd begun to believe that he was right, that she would be able to do this and come out safely at the other end. 'It's no good. There's a blockage in the way.'

She was almost certain that she heard him swear at the other end and realised that she must actually have been nearing the end of her journey before she'd come to her enforced halt because radio reception was becoming much clearer.

Was this where it was all going to end? Was she finally going to have to find out whether she had the courage to end things cleanly, or would she chicken out and force Adam to listen to her deteriorate as dehydration took its fatal toll? One thing she knew was that she wouldn't be able to make herself switch the radio off. She would want to be able to hear his voice until the last possible moment. Or would the battery die before then?

'Maggie, how big are the rocks and how many of them are there?' Adam demanded, dragging her out of her spiralling thoughts and sending her off in another direction.

'Does it matter?' she said, unable to care that she sounded utterly defeated. 'I can hardly go around them.'

She'd managed to stay upbeat all the way

through her mother's treatment without once cracking, knowing she needed to borrow her strength. Now she just didn't seem to be able to find anything left to dredge up for herself.

'Of course it matters!' he snapped. 'You might not be able to go around them, but they might be able to go around you.'

'What?' Her brain was too tired to work out what he'd just said.

'*Keresik*, listen to me,' he said patiently. 'If the blockage is a small one, with relatively small rocks, you should be able to pass them past your body one by one until your way is clear again. Now, have another look and tell me what you see.'

'Some of them are quite big,' she said when she'd had a closer look. 'But the ones they're holding up look relatively small.'

Even so, the sheer quantity of them was daunting. It would take so long to move them all, one at a time, dragging, rolling, pushing and sliding to pass them through the tiny space between the softness of her body and the immovability of the granite surrounding her.

She hardly dared to allow herself to hope that this wasn't the disaster it had looked at first sight. The prospect nearly had her sobbing with frustration, but the only way she would know if the job was possible was if she did what she'd had to do ever since this whole incident had begun…take everything one step at a time, one rock at a time, until she discovered what she could achieve.

And with Adam waiting for her, bullying her into continuing the fight, even as he encouraged her, how could she *not* give it her best effort?

CHAPTER TEN

'I'VE done it!' Maggie exulted as she finally pushed the last rock past her hip and forced herself forward, ignoring the fact that she'd just gathered a few new bruises.

'Good girl,' Adam praised softly, but she was beyond telling him off. 'I *knew* you could do it,' he added, and suddenly she was sure he meant it because he'd *always* believed in her, right from when they'd been teenagers.

What she didn't know was why—after all, he'd been nearly three years older when their friendship had first started, and to teenagers that could be a gap as vast as an ocean, especially when the older one was about to leave to begin professional training.

Well, if—*when*—she got out of there, she thought with new determination, she was going to make sure that she asked him exactly what he'd seen in the skinny little girl she'd been, but that sort of conversation was going to have to wait until she'd had about a gallon of water to drink, something hot to eat and the longest, deepest, hottest bath she could find, with about a yard of scented bubbles on the top, because otherwise she was going to be so stiff and sore in the morning and...

As she reached her hand forward again she caught sight of the time and groaned aloud when she realised that it already *was* morning.

In fact, in about half an hour it was going to be sunrise and time she would normally be getting up to get ready to go to work to start her next shift.

'Maggie? *Keresik?*' Adam called, and it took a moment for her to realise why his voice sounded different.

'Adam! I can hear you!' she exclaimed. 'I can hear you without the radio. How far away are you?' Her hands were suddenly shaking so much that it was almost impossible for her to find the switch on the torch to turn it off.

And there it was—not just the vague glimmer of light at the end of the tunnel that there should have been this early in the morning but the biggest, brightest most beautiful glare that she'd ever seen that told her that the generator had been moved and there were people up there, waiting to help her.

That was the moment that told her that the end of her ordeal was in sight, and the sense of relief that hit her was so powerful that for several long moments she was totally unable to move a muscle.

'Come on, Maggie the Mole. Don't be frightened of the lights,' he murmured softly into the radio, rather than calling down to her for everyone to hear, almost as though he was trying to coax a shy animal into the open. 'Come on up so I can collect the hug I've been waiting for all night.'

'You might not want to hug me when you see

how dirty I am,' she warned as she started moving again, her arms and legs feeling strangely leaden so that she had to force them into dragging her body over those last few remaining yards.

'I'll take my chances,' he promised with a smile in his voice that she couldn't wait to see in person.

And then, suddenly, she was emerging from the top of the ventilation shaft and there were hands reaching for her from every direction, grabbing her sore elbows and making her squeak with pain until Adam growled at them to let her go. And then he wrapped his arms tightly around her, surrounding her with his own warmth, and was lifting her completely off her feet and whirling her round and round in a kaleidoscope of light and laughter and applause.

She was totally unable to hear a single word he was saying because of the voices around them and she had no idea why the lights seemed to be flashing until Adam finally lowered her to her feet and she realised that there must have been a dozen people pressing towards them with

what looked like a forest of cameras and micro-
phones all pointing in her direction.

'Maggie!'

'Miss Pascoe!'

'Over here, Maggie!'

It was a good job that he had his arm wrapped
around her shoulders to steady her or she would
have fallen over with shock.

'What are all these people doing here?' she
asked, then didn't care what his answer was
when he smiled at her like that.

'Do you want me to get rid of them?' he asked
with a devilish glint in his eye.

'Please!' She glanced down at herself and
could have cried when she saw the state of her
uniform, the smart green she'd always worn
with pride now dusty, stained and torn. 'I look
disgusting, and they're all taking photos!' she
wailed, burying her face against the shoulder of
his borrowed jacket. He laughed aloud before
he held up a commanding hand.

As if by magic, the cacophony died away until
there was only the steady thrum of the genera-

tor powering the lights and a few indignant calls from the birds that had been woken too soon by the artificial dawn.

'As you can all see,' Adam said, his strong voice carrying easily right to the back of the crowd laying siege to them, 'Maggie's out and she's safe and well. We'll be saying a special thank you to all the rescue crew in the Penhally Arms this evening, but for now she just needs a little time to catch her breath.'

He started to turn away, wrapping the blanket he was handed around her shoulders to shelter her from the sharp breeze blowing in from the ocean below, before tucking her against his side with what felt like an extremely possessive arm.

Behind them there was a renewed storm of shouting when the media circus realised that they'd just neatly been balked of an immediate interview with her, but there was an impressive wall of rescue squad personnel wearing high-visibility clothing standing guard, preventing them from getting any closer.

Not that Maggie felt she had anything much to say.

She'd only been doing what a paramedic was trained to do when she'd stabilised Tel and prepared him for transport to St Piran's, and it had just been common sense to escort the other lads out to the surface when she'd had to collect more supplies.

As for her journey up the ventilation shaft… the only remarkable thing about that was the fact that Adam had been able to persuade her to attempt it in the first place.

'Maggie?' The young voice was accompanied by the feeling of someone tugging on her tattered sleeve, and she turned to find Jem Althorp standing there with his mother.

'Jem! And Kate!' she exclaimed in surprise. 'I thought you'd both be back home by now, tucked up in bed.'

'I couldn't go to sleep,' Jem said earnestly. 'Not until I knew they'd got you out of the mine safely.'

'I took him home to feed him and get him clean and warm, but we couldn't stay there, knowing you were still down the mine. We both wanted to be here,' Kate said. 'I *had* to be here to thank you for looking after him for me, and…and to apologise for shouting at you earlier. I—'

'Kate, don't worry about it. Just take him home and put it all behind you,' she advised. 'You've got a remarkably brave boy there, and he deserves a medal for staying down there with Tel.'

All the while they had been talking, Adam had been edging her gently away from the noise and the people until they'd said their goodbyes. Then he quickened his pace, leading her along the grassy slope and through the gate at the far side of the field until the lights and the people were left behind, the intrusive cameras kept firmly at bay by the determined efforts of the rescue squad, who had been there almost from the beginning of her ordeal.

In the shelter of a solid Cornish stone hedge he finally drew her down to sit beside him on the short-cropped grass and a tiny corner of her mind reasoned that there must have been a flock of sheep there until recently. Had they been taken to a field closer to the farmhouse ready for lambing?

'Here,' Adam said. 'You're probably ready for this.' He held out a bottle of water.

'Oh, yes!' she said, suddenly realising just how dry her throat was, and reached for it, only to realise that her battered and bruised fingers were too sore to unscrew the top.

'Ah, *keresik*, let me do that for you,' he offered with a catch in his voice as he took the top off and handed it to her.

'Oh, that tastes so good,' she said when the cool liquid had slid down her throat. 'I don't think I've ever been so thirsty.'

'Is there anything in your pack that I can put on your hands for you?'

'My pack!' She'd completely forgotten that she'd been dragging that up the shaft with her, attached by what was now a very dirty length of bandage.

She suddenly started to laugh as a ridiculous image leapt into her mind.

'What's so funny?' he asked with a frown,

clearly wondering if she'd finally cracked under the strain.

'I'd completely forgotten about my pack…that I'd tied it to me… And if you hadn't seen it before you swung me round…' She laughed helplessly.

'We wouldn't have had any difficulty getting rid of the press because I'd have flattened the lot of them with it.' His deeper laughter joined hers in joyous early-morning harmony as the day brightened steadily around them. 'I couldn't believe how heavy it was. What do you paramedics keep in there? Bricks?'

Suddenly Maggie remembered putting the souvenir pieces of rock in the pack before she'd started that last climb and reached for the appropriate pocket.

Adam had to take over when her fingers were too clumsy to open it but then she burrowed down inside until she felt the rough texture of the two rocks and pulled the bigger one out into the strengthening light.

'Not bricks exactly,' she said. 'But just before I started climbing that awful ventilation shaft I saw this and thought it would be a pretty memento. Do you recognise what it is? Isn't that what they call Fool's gold because so many people mistake it for the real thing?'

Adam examined it, turning the heavily streaked rock over and over in his hands.

'It might be an idea to show it Young George,' he suggested with a strange little smile.

'Well, he does know more than most about the mines around here,' she agreed easily. 'He'll enjoy a chuckle when he realises that the only bit of treasure I salvaged from my time down there was a bit of iron pyrites.'

'It could be.' But he was still smiling mysteriously as he continued. 'Young George and I were talking when you were asleep. He'd had a chance to look at the old map and it reminded him that the mine's original name was Wheal Owr. That was corrupted over the years and ended up being anglicised to Wheal Owl.'

'So, does *owr* mean owl?' She was always interested in anything to do with the history of the region.

'No. Apparently owl is *kowann* in Cornish.'

'So *owr* is…?'

'Gold,' he said with a significant glance at the rock in his hand. 'The mine was originally called Wheal Gold and it looks as if you brought up a piece of the evidence as to why it got its name.'

'You're kidding!' she exclaimed, and traced a bright vein with a tentative fingertip.

'I wonder,' Adam said reflectively as he turned it over in his hand. 'Do you think there would be enough in here for a wedding ring…or two?'

'A wedding ring?' Maggie wasn't sure what she was hearing. It had been a very long night and she could easily be hallucinating or…

'Is it such a hard question, *keresik*?'

She wouldn't have believed that he could sound so uncertain. When he'd been eighteen he had seemed to have all the answers and a year ago…

'While I was…down there…you said Caroline was in a coma. So how long was it before…?'

'She'd already been comatose for months by then, but her mother just couldn't let go, couldn't bear to lose her only daughter when she looked as if there was absolutely nothing wrong with her…as if she'd just wake up at any moment.'

Now she could see that the shadows she'd glimpsed in his eyes were sadness and regret for a wasted life.

'I suppose I felt guilty because I'd never really loved her, so I just let her mother go on hoping but…' He shook his head. 'I couldn't let it go on any longer, not after I'd seen you again and realised just what had been missing in my life all that time.'

He took one of her grubby, scraped hands in his and held it gently against his face, a full day's growth of prickly dark beard making him look like the perfect illustration of a pirate.

'It took me a while to persuade Caroline's mother that it was time to let go, and then there was my contract to work out, but I knew what I wanted—to come back to Penhally and persuade you that you still loved me enough to give me a second chance. What I didn't know was whether you'd allow me to get close enough to explain where everything had gone wrong.'

'And within minutes of setting eyes on you, I'm trapped down a mine and a captive audience,' she said wryly, loving the way his eyes gleamed in the light of the new day. 'Did you really mean it? That you wanted to move back to Penhally? I thought you were only here as a locum?'

'They're desperately short of staff, with two of them disappearing off to Italy last month. I'm here as a short-term locum and there's a retired GP from another practice who's been helping out. So there's a permanent position for me at Penhally Bay Surgery if I want it, but I wasn't going to commit myself to it in case you didn't want to have anything more to do with me. It would have been too painful to see you and not—'

'You mean, you wouldn't have tried to change my mind?' she teased.

'Of course I would,' he said very seriously. 'I meant what I said when you were down there—

that you had to get out of there safely because I need you in my life as much as I need air to breathe. And I would love to settle in Penhally permanently with you…unless you'd rather go somewhere else?'

'It might seem rather unadventurous, but I like living here,' she said, while the realisation was slowly dawning that he might really have meant that comment about the wedding rings to be the forerunner of a proposal. Or had he?

'That's not to say that I wouldn't like to travel abroad at some stage,' she added uncertainly, not really knowing where this conversation was going. Was he just asking if she'd mind if he moved back to Penhally, that it wouldn't matter to her if she saw him around the place on a daily basis? 'Um, the furthest I've been from home was that course in London.'

'In which case, I'll accept the permanent position,' he said with a new sense of purpose in his voice, 'but I'll work to the end of my present contract first—that will take me to the end of March. Then I'll start the new one at the beginning of May. That means I'll be giving the practice nearly a month and a half's notice that I'm going to be away on my honeymoon for the whole of April. Well, at least they'll know that I'm going to be back full time before the summer visitors start flooding into Cornwall and the practice goes manic. But perhaps you'd rather wait?' he added hastily, so he must have seen the frown of puzzlement on her face.

'Wait for what?' she asked. 'I'm sorry, Adam, but my mind must be fuzzy with lack of sleep. What would I be waiting for?'

'Oh, *keresik*, have I done everything wrong?' he demanded, looking quite stricken. 'Here I am asking whether you'd rather wait a few more months and be a June bride when I haven't even proposed properly.'

'Proposed?' she whispered, wide-eyed as he suddenly shifted to his knees on the grass in front of her.

He was still wearing his ruined trousers and the borrowed jacket from one of the rescue team but he'd never looked more handsome to her.

The pale February sun was just creeping over the field behind her to outline the face of the man she'd loved ever since she'd been fifteen, and the wide expanse of the ocean beyond the safe harbour of Penhally Bay was spread out behind him as he carefully took both her hands in his.

'*Keresik*, I can't remember a time when I didn't love you, and I know I'll love you for the rest of my life, so will you do me the honour of marrying me?'

'Oh, Adam, yes, please. I love you, too,' she whispered, and had to swallow hard to stop the happy tears spoiling the moment. Besides, she had something important to add. 'And I don't want to be a June bride because that's too far away. I've been waiting to marry you since my sixteenth birthday.'

'So let's not wait at all,' he suggested, drawing her up to her knees so that they were facing each other before he said solemnly, 'I, Adam Donnelly, take you, Margaret Pascoe, to be my lawful wedded wife, to have and to hold from this day forward as long as we both shall live.'

Maggie knew that they would have the formal legalisation of their vows in the presence of their friends later, but she also knew that nothing could be more solemn or binding than becoming his bride in the soft grey sunrise of a Cornish February morning.

She smiled into those beautiful dark blue eyes and her heart swelled with happiness as she said, 'I, Margaret Pascoe, take you, Adam Donnelly to be my lawful wedded husband, to have and to hold from this day forward as long as we both shall live.'

'May I kiss my bride?' he asked softly, but before she could answer a sudden gust of wind buffeted them and brought the first sharp needles of rain with them.

'Your bride would love a kiss, but wonders if she could have it somewhere just a little bit warmer,' she said, as the blanket was flipped off her shoulders by the next gust and her teeth started to chatter. 'It seems as if that rain might be arriving a bit sooner than forecast.'

'Going somewhere warmer—and more

private—sounds like a wonderful idea, especially for what I've got in mind,' he agreed, as he rescued the blanket and helped her to her feet, then grinned. 'Your place is closer. I hope your shower is big enough for two.' And he swung her up into his arms, travel-stained pack and all.

She squealed in surprise at his unexpected move, then laughed as she flung her arms around those broad shoulders and tucked her head where it had always belonged—beside his.

She'd thought he would stride swiftly back to the field that had been the scene of so much drama during the night, to the car he'd left there when he'd come to help find the boys, but instead he paused to gaze down at her for a long moment.

'Ah, Maggie, *keresik*, I can't tell you how glad I am to have you safely in my arms again,' he said, tightening them around her and pressing his cheek against hers. '*And* how impossible it is to wait before I have at least one kiss,' he growled in her ear, before he pressed hungry lips to hers.

And suddenly it didn't matter that the wind

was getting stronger, colder and wetter. All that mattered was that she was in his arms and that this was the start of the rest of their lives…together.

MEDICAL™

—⩗— *Large Print* —⩗—

Titles for the next six months…

September

THE SURGEON'S FATHERHOOD SURPRISE Jennifer Taylor
THE ITALIAN SURGEON CLAIMS HIS Alison Roberts
BRIDE
DESERT DOCTOR, SECRET SHEIKH Meredith Webber
A WEDDING IN WARRAGURRA Fiona Lowe
THE FIREFIGHTER AND THE SINGLE MUM Laura Iding
THE NURSE'S LITTLE MIRACLE Molly Evans

October

THE DOCTOR'S ROYAL LOVE-CHILD Kate Hardy
HIS ISLAND BRIDE Marion Lennox
A CONSULTANT BEYOND COMPARE Joanna Neil
THE SURGEON BOSS'S BRIDE Melanie Milburne
A WIFE WORTH WAITING FOR Maggie Kingsley
DESERT PRINCE, EXPECTANT MOTHER Olivia Gates

November

NURSE BRIDE, BAYSIDE WEDDING Gill Sanderson
BILLIONAIRE DOCTOR, ORDINARY Carol Marinelli
NURSE
THE SHEIKH SURGEON'S BABY Meredith Webber
THE OUTBACK DOCTOR'S SURPRISE BRIDE Amy Andrews
A WEDDING AT LIMESTONE COAST Lucy Clark
THE DOCTOR'S MEANT-TO-BE MARRIAGE Janice Lynn

MILLS & BOON®
Pure reading pleasure™   0808 LP 2P P1 Medical

MEDICAL™

 *Large Print*

December

SINGLE DAD SEEKS A WIFE — Melanie Milburne
HER FOUR-YEAR BABY SECRET — Alison Roberts
COUNTRY DOCTOR, SPRING BRIDE — Abigail Gordon
MARRYING THE RUNAWAY BRIDE — Jennifer Taylor
THE MIDWIFE'S BABY — Fiona McArthur
THE FATHERHOOD MIRACLE — Margaret Barker

January

VIRGIN MIDWIFE, PLAYBOY DOCTOR — Margaret McDonagh
THE REBEL DOCTOR'S BRIDE — Sarah Morgan
THE SURGEON'S SECRET BABY WISH — Laura Iding
PROPOSING TO THE CHILDREN'S DOCTOR — Joanna Neil
EMERGENCY: WIFE NEEDED — Emily Forbes
ITALIAN DOCTOR, FULL-TIME FATHER — Dianne Drake

February

THEIR MIRACLE BABY — Caroline Anderson
THE CHILDREN'S DOCTOR AND THE SINGLE MUM — Lilian Darcy
THE SPANISH DOCTOR'S LOVE-CHILD — Kate Hardy
PREGNANT NURSE, NEW-FOUND FAMILY — Lynne Marshall
HER VERY SPECIAL BOSS — Anne Fraser
THE GP'S MARRIAGE WISH — Judy Campbell

MILLS & BOON®
Pure reading pleasure™

0808 LP 2P P2 Medical